School Friends

Secrets, hopes and dreams…
School friends are for ever!

Collect the whole **School Friends** series:

Party at Silver Spires
Dancer at Silver Spires
Dreams at Silver Spires
Magic at Silver Spires
Success at Silver Spires
Mystery at Silver Spires

...all featuring the Emerald dorm girls

First Term at Silver Spires
Drama at Silver Spires
Rivalry at Silver Spires
Princess at Silver Spires
Secrets at Silver Spires
Star of Silver Spires

...all featuring the Amethyst dorm girls

Want to know more about **School Friends**?
Check out
www.silverspiresschool.co.uk

Dancer
at
Silver
Spires

Ann Bryant

USBORNE

For Lynne Benton, with love.
Thank you for your support.

First published in the UK in 2010 by Usborne Publishing Ltd.,
Usborne House, 83-85 Saffron Hill, London EC1N 8RT, England.
www.usborne.com

Cover illustration by Rui Ricardo for folioart.co.uk

The name Usborne and the devices 🔱 🎈 are Trade Marks of
Usborne Publishing Ltd.

A CIP catalogue record for this book is available from the British Library.

JFMAMJJASON /10 95196 ISBN 9780746098653
Printed in Reading, Berkshire, UK.

Chapter One

I stared around the dining hall and thought for at least the hundredth time how much I love it here at Silver Spires. I suppose all boarding schools are great, but I just don't see how they can be as great as this one. I mean, I was so nervous when I started here eight weeks ago, but the very first time I came into this dining hall with the other five girls from my dormitory, I felt so happy. It was obvious we were going to get on with each other. Well, it's true I did feel a bit anxious about Antonia, who's Italian, and Nicole, who's amazingly clever. Those two didn't seem to hit it off as well as the rest of us, but

I felt sure it would work out eventually because they both seemed so nice. And I was right. They're best friends now.

My own best friend is called Sasha, and while I was staring around right then, she was listening intently to something that Emily was telling her. Even though Emily's story seemed to be going on and on, and personally I tuned out ages before, Sasha still looked interested. She kept nodding slowly, her big blue eyes looking straight at Emily. And that's because Sasha is such a fantastic listener. I'm so glad we're best friends.

As soon as lunch was over we all set off through the grounds for afternoon lessons. It was maths first, and that's one of the three subjects we've been put in sets for, which means that we six friends aren't all together for those lessons, like we are for everything else.

"See you later!" called Antonia, as she went off with Emily and Emily's best friend, Bryony.

"I can't believe how good Antonia's getting at English!" said Sasha. "And her English accent's getting better too."

"I know!" said Nicole, looking happy. "And it's great that she's been put up a set for maths and science."

I nodded. "If she carries on going up, you two might be together in top sets for everything before the end of Year Seven!"

Nicole laughed. "That would be really good," she said, linking arms with me on one side and Sasha on the other and falling into step with us. But almost immediately she pulled away, half laughing. "Do you know, I always feel a bit like an elephant when I'm walking beside you, Izzy!"

Sasha laughed too. "I know exactly what you mean!"

My body slumped instinctively as the little voice in my head started up. *Not this again.*

Nicole must have sensed my dejection. "Oh, Izzy, it's a compliment, you know," she said. "You're just so graceful."

Sasha grinned at me. "Except when you deliberately don't stand up straight, like right now."

"I'd love to have great posture, like you," Nicole added.

I tried to smile while my mind searched around for a quick way of getting off this terrible subject, and the voice in my head grew louder. *I don't want to talk about being graceful and standing up straight. I don't even want to think about it. I know where it leads.*

"You'd make a great dancer, Izzy," said Sasha.

I didn't reply because I couldn't think of what to say. We'd had this kind of conversation lots of times since I'd started at Silver Spires and no one knew how much I hated it. Well, actually that's not true. I thought Sasha was starting to notice how uncomfortable I got whenever anyone mentioned me in the same breath as dancing or ballet, and how I always tried to quickly change the conversation. The trouble is, Sasha's such a good listener that I'm afraid one of these days I might be tempted to tell her about my past. But it's a secret. If I told her about the *other me*, she'd think I was completely mad.

And just when I was thinking about my past an annoying voice popped into my head. *Is it that she'll think you're mad, or just that you can't ever let yourself talk about it?*

Suddenly I felt shaky. The truth had finally hit me.

It's not that I won't talk about it, it's that I *can't*.

As soon as afternoon school was finished, we six went back to our boarding house, Forest Ash, to drop our stuff off in our dorm. Forest Ash is quite a modern house, not like Hazeldean and Willowhaven, but it's the best because we've got the nicest staff. The other three houses are called Oakley, Beech House and Elmhurst. On the days we don't do an after-school club we get to have free time before supper, and it's always a great part of the day because you can stop concentrating after all the lessons, and do anything you want. I was looking forward to having some time on my own, but Nicole and Antonia were trying to persuade me and Sasha to go to debating club with them.

"Eet ees such good fun!" said Antonia, her Italian accent coming through strongly. It often does when she's excited.

"We can't just turn up, can we?" said Sasha.

Nicole nodded hard. "Yes, you can. No one would mind, I'm sure." She sounded so bright and breezy. "Go on, give it a try. I bet you'd really like it."

"Shall we?" asked Sasha, turning to me, eyes dancing.

"I'm not sure..." I began, wondering how to explain that I'd really rather just be on my own with my thoughts for a while. "Why don't you go, Sasha?"

A cloud seemed to cross her sunny face. "Are you sure? I won't go if you don't want me to."

I smiled and spoke quickly. "No, it's fine, honestly. I don't feel like sitting still, that's all."

Antonia grinned. "I theenk you are going to walk and get the energy out of your legs, yes?"

I nodded and smiled back. My friends all know I'm not very good at sitting still for long periods of time, and it's almost become a joke amongst us. At the end of lessons Emily and I are always the first out, and if we go anywhere on the school minibus or the coach, the others let us get off before them so we can feel free. With Em, it's more that she wants to be out in the fresh air as she feels stifled indoors. But with me it's because I want to move around. "Izzy whizzy makes me dizzy!" Sasha once said, and the whizzy soon got shortened to Whizz and kind of stuck as a nickname for me that my friends all use occasionally.

As soon as they'd left the dorm I took the pile of ballet photos and programmes and cuttings and other souvenirs from my bottom drawer and climbed up the ladder to sit on my bed. I love the way we've all got our own little space in this dorm. In fact I love the dorm, full stop. Every Year Seven dorm is named after a precious stone and ours is called Emerald. We're lucky because it's quite a big dorm and each of us has a cabin bed with a desk area underneath where we keep our bits and pieces, plus there are some drawers and a wardrobe. We've also all got a little light built into our headboards so we can read in bed, as well as a pinboard each that we can decorate how we want. Mine's covered with photos of my mum and dad and my big brother, Max, with his girlfriend, Claire, and my little sister, Holly. They're mainly photos of our last summer holiday together. It feels like Claire's one of the family now. She and Max have been going out for over a year and I really like her because she treats me like a friend and not like Max's little sister.

From where I was sitting on my bed I could see Emily's pinboard right opposite, every single centimetre taken up with pictures of her beloved horse and all sorts of plants and shrubs and trees in her farm garden back home in Ireland. I think Emily loves to see things growing as much as I secretly love ballet. Only it's a different kind of love. Hers seems so straightforward, and mine is so...complicated.

I looked at the picture on the top of the pile I was holding. It was a signed photo of the famous ballerina from The Royal Ballet, Alina Cojocaru. She was in the costume of the title role in *Ondine*. That's one of my favourite ballets. I spent ages staring at the picture while my mind flooded with muddled thoughts about how much I used to adore every single thing to do with ballet, including actually dancing myself. *Especially* dancing myself. But the sadness always hits me when I remind myself that I'm not as good at ballet as I thought. And that's why I'm trying to get all thoughts about it out of my system, to stop the hurt that overwhelms me every time I remember what a failure I am.

I turned to the next picture, which was of my old ballet teacher, Miss Amelia. She wasn't in any particular ballet pose, but you could still tell she was a dancer just from the way she was standing. I swallowed and bit my lip as I looked at her smiling at me from the photo. I must have disappointed her so much when she put me in for the audition at the very best ballet school in Great Britain, The Royal Ballet School, and I didn't get in. She pretended not to be upset, for my sake, but I knew she was really.

After I'd had the terrible news that I'd failed the entrance exam, I couldn't stop crying. Mum couldn't comfort me and in the end she took me to see Miss Amelia at her house. I remember how Miss Amelia kept on patting me on the back and saying soothing words that didn't actually soothe me at all: "I know it's a terrible blow, but you'll get over it, Izzy." And

I just sat there staring blankly ahead, all my crying leaving me so tired and small. "Just try to relax and enjoy your Easter holiday now," she went on in the same gentle voice. "By next term you'll be back to your usual self, you'll see!"

But I wasn't. In fact I don't know how I got through the summer term at all. Well, that's not quite true. I got through it because of Silver Spires. Mum and Dad had said I should apply here too – "just in case" – and after The Royal Ballet School news, I was *so* glad I'd been accepted. Knowing that I would be coming to this amazing boarding school made up for some of my failure, and I put all my energy into thinking about coming here instead of where I thought I'd be going. I spent ages making plans about what I'd bring, and imagining how my new life would be.

I loved this school right from the introductory day at the end of the summer term. That day feels like a bit of a dream now, and I know I didn't take everything in. But it filled up my mind, and when I got home I drew a big line under my other life. I decided to give up going to ballet classes with Miss Amelia and made the decision that ballet would be in my past, belonging to the *other me*. I wouldn't talk about it – ever. The door to The Royal Ballet School might have shut in my face, but the Silver Spires door had opened, and when I walked through it at the beginning of this term, I shut the door to my old life firmly behind me to keep it out.

The trouble is, however firmly I thought I'd closed the door on my past, it kept on opening of its own accord and letting bits of my secret life come in, confusing and upsetting me. And all these ballet keepsakes don't help. I should never have brought them with me. This was the third time I'd taken my little pile of photos and things out to have a look at, and each time I'd felt upset. I decided to put it all away and go for a walk round Silver Spires. That always makes me feel better.

But I didn't get very far, because there's something about the banister that runs along the landing outside our dorm that pulls mc like a magnet back into the world of ballet whenever I see it. It reminds me so strongly of a *barre*, the wooden handrail that goes round the walls of every single ballet studio. If I'm with Sasha and the others I make sure I don't look at it, but sometimes, on my own, I simply can't resist it, and right now was one of those times.

I looked around, then leaned over the banister to check there was no one on their way upstairs. Then I placed my hand slowly and lightly on the rail and stood as I've stood so often at the beginning of my ballet class, tall and straight, ribs pulled up, shoulders down, feet and legs turned right out in first position. I felt as though I'd hear Miss Amelia's voice at any second. *Imagine the invisible string, girls, pulling right through from the bottom of your spine to the top of your head and drawing you closer to the ceiling. And when you can't grow any taller, then you are ready to begin your steps.*

I carefully started to bend my knees in a *plié*, which is always the first exercise we do at the *barre*, but there was a noise behind me, and I had to pull clumsily out of my shape and grope around on the floor pretending I'd dropped something. Then I quickly stood up and looked around. It must have been one of those creaks that all silent buildings seem to have, because there was no one about.

The spell of my imaginary ballet class had been broken though, so I started to walk downstairs with heavy footsteps. But the frustration of not even finishing that *plié* got worse and worse, so when I was halfway down I made the mistake of looking back up, and of course my eye caught the banister again, and a moment later I found myself leaping back up to it, two steps at a time. It wasn't just that I hadn't finished the *plié*, it was because I could have done it better. My insteps had definitely rolled slightly and that should never happen.

Holding the banister lightly, I got into first position even more carefully than the last time, and once I'd imagined Miss Amelia counting the pianist in, I was ready to start again. All my attention was on my left instep. And so was Miss Amelia's. Her voice seemed so clear now. *No rolling the feet, girls. Pull back.* But the moment I did that, my arms and back felt stiff. And when I relaxed them, my feet went wrong again. What was the matter with me?

I snapped my legs straight and walked downstairs and out of Forest Ash without looking back. It was no wonder I'd failed to get into The Royal Ballet School, and no wonder I'd never be a professional ballerina. I was nowhere near the right standard if I couldn't even do a proper *plié*.

It's horrible when I have these feelings and I knew I had to shake them away before Sasha and the others got back from their clubs and we all went to supper. Otherwise everyone would want to know what was the matter with me, and there was no way I'd ever be able to explain how unbearable it is to fail at the very thing you want to do best, and to know that your dreams can never ever come true because of that failure. Maybe I should have gone to debating club after all. That would have made me focus on something completely different and got rid of the turmoil in my head. But it was too late now. I'd probably be interrupting them right in the middle of an important discussion. Perhaps I'd go to the big main library instead. There's a lovely peaceful atmosphere in there and everyone is quiet and in their own little world. Yes, that's what I'd do.

But even as I was having these thoughts, my feet were taking me of their own accord towards the sports complex, and when I got there I walked straight past the big sports hall, and then past the small hall, to the room at the end. The dance studio. I just wanted to remind myself what it looked like, because I hadn't seen it since my introductory day when my parents and I had been shown round.

The Deputy Head, Mrs. Andrews, had taken us into the sports hall, and we'd stayed there for ages while she'd talked about all the many different sports and PE activities at Silver Spires. Then she'd said, "And now for the dance studio..." She'd turned to me. "I don't know if you're into dance, Izzy, but we have all sorts of clubs you can join – tap, ballet, jazz...lots." I'd given her the tiniest shake of the head and hoped like mad that Mum wouldn't say anything, and she didn't, thank goodness. But she'd exchanged a look with Dad and sighed as though I was a hopeless case. So Mrs. Andrews had suggested we just had a quick look. She'd pointed out the sprung floor and the double *barres* around three of the four walls. She didn't need to. I'd already noticed absolutely everything about that studio in one glance and it had brought all my past flooding back and made me feel trapped. It was such a relief when we finally left the sports centre and my heartbeat had slowed down to normal.

And now here I was again, peering into the gloom of the empty room, because it was late afternoon and practically dark outside, which meant I could only see it by the light from the corridor. I pressed down on the door handle and felt relieved that it was locked as I'd thought it would be. But even without going in, the sight of the studio made my heart bump. I wasn't sure if I was nervous or scared or anxious or excited or a mixture of all those things. All I knew was that the feeling was too much and I had to get away quickly, so I rushed out of the sports complex and headed back to the common room at Forest Ash.

I'd watch TV until six thirty when it was supper time. Yes, that's what I'd do.

* * *

I'd never been in the common room without at least one of my friends with me, and I felt a bit funny being there on my own. It's a very large room with a TV and a DVD player, and plenty of sofas and comfy chairs and beanbags. Surprisingly there were only two Year Ten girls in there, called Olivia and Maria, sitting at the table round the corner from the TV area. To tell the truth, I was a bit scared of them, because they always seemed so aloof. I switched on the telly, then flopped down on one of the lovely squishy beanbags, only to hear Maria say, "The choreography's going to be so amazing!"

I nearly got up and went straight out again at the sound of that word, but I didn't because the girls might have thought I was weird. So instead I tried with all my might to block out what I'd just heard and to concentrate on the TV programme. I couldn't do it, though. The *other me* was sitting up straight, filled with curiosity.

Choreography is like a composition, but of a dance rather than a piece of music. And the *other me* was desperate to know if the choreography they were talking about was for a ballet, or for a different kind of dance.

"We'll need to get in as much practice and as many rehearsals as we can, you know," said Maria.

There was a pause and I imagined Olivia nodding.

Then after a moment Maria spoke again. "Abi's really good, isn't she? I wish I could dance as well as her."

"Abi's not that much better than...us two, actually," Olivia answered quickly, and I heard big irritation in her voice.

"No," said Maria lightly, "but I mean us three are way better than the other four in the group anyway, aren't we?"

"Obviously."

I didn't like the sound of that *obviously*. It was hard and boastful.

When neither of them spoke for a while, I presumed that was the end of the conversation and I sank lower into the beanbag, beginning to relax again. But then I nearly shot out of it altogether at the sound of Maria's voice.

"Miss Morgan's right, isn't she? I mean it's much harder to make ballet look good onstage, compared to any other type of dance, isn't it? Unless you're a professional ballet dancer, I guess."

My heart began to thud. They were talking about a ballet performance. Miss Morgan? Yes, I'd heard of her. She was the Silver Spires dance mistress.

What? A ballet performance? Here? At school? said the *other me*, forgetting, as usual, that the *new me* didn't want to know these things.

And a few seconds later Olivia gave me the answer. She sounded half nervous, half sulky. "It's going to be so scary on that stage when just about everyone in this place thinks ballet is the least cool thing ever. They just don't get it, do they? I mean, they've got no clue how hard it is."

I didn't stay to hear any more. I just got up, switched off the TV and left the room. I wished I'd never found out about this ballet performance. The very thought of it made waves of tension zap through me. I knew it had nothing to do with me. It wasn't as if I'd be dancing myself. But it was still ballet, and that wasn't supposed to be a part of my new life here at Silver Spires. I'd done everything I could to avoid it, yet it had crept up on me again.

I raced up to the dorm and sat on my bed, trying to calm down, telling myself that I didn't have to watch the performance if I didn't want to. Surely it wouldn't be compulsory to attend. In fact, I didn't even know if Year Sevens would be invited. No, I'd just keep right away from it and everything would be fine.

But the *other me* wouldn't leave the subject alone.

It sounds like Abi's really good. I'd like to see her dance.

Then the *new me* slammed the door shut. *Well, you're not going to. It would only upset you. Ballet's in your past.*

Chapter Two

"**O**kay, girls, let's do some stretches. Sitting on your mats in your proper gym position." Mrs. Truman, our PE teacher, paused and checked we all had legs stretched, toes pointed, backs straight and heads up. "Remember, gymnastics is an individual sport, so you don't need to look around at each other."

We were all still puffing a bit from the warm-up. We'd done lots of side skipping and different sorts of jogging with our heels up and then our knees up, and backwards jogging too, and all the activities made me feel alive. Gym is the complete opposite to ballet. In gym, you don't turn out your legs and your feet like you do in ballet. You point your feet straight out in front. You don't curve your arms softly, you snap them tight in a wide V. You don't grow up out of your ribcage, feeling the imaginary piece of string making you tall; you arch your back hard. If I'd gone to The Royal Ballet School I wouldn't be allowed to do gym, because it would spoil my ballet technique and risk injury. At Silver Spires, I can do it as much as I want. So I make the most of it and, as well as the ordinary lessons, I go to gym club.

After the stretches, we put the mats together and worked in groups on a routine which had to include moves from four to three to two points of balance. I was with all my friends and we had a brilliant time moving in and out of various shapes. I concentrated hard on making sure I didn't do anything that might look too graceful or ballet-like, and didn't mind too much when Bryony suddenly said, "Your legs are very strong, aren't they?"

"I like gym," I said, carefully.

Bryony was looking at me as though she was really impressed with my strength. "You're the only one of us six who can support my weight in the aeroplane balance," she said now. "And yet you've got such a small, slim build. Have you done lots of gym before, Izzy?"

I felt myself crumble a bit inside. "No, not loads...well, quite a lot..." I knew I was sounding unsure of myself and it was a relief when Emily suddenly spoke excitedly. "Let's compare thigh muscles! Mine are really strong because of horse riding."

But then Mrs. Truman clapped her hands to bring us all to attention. "Good work, everyone. Well done! Sit down now and I'll tell you about the dance show that's happening on the second-to-last Saturday evening of term."

I felt a gasp inside me. Why was Mrs. Truman telling us about the dance show? What did it have to do with us? This had been such a good gym lesson until now.

"This is a show for the whole school, which means that anyone can be in it. And we also need a nice big audience to help create a brilliant atmosphere. There aren't any parents or outsiders at this event, but last year the whole school came along and had a great time!"

"What kind of dancing is it?" someone asked.

"Well I'm just coming to that," said Mrs. Truman. "If you're keen on doing a tap routine, or modern dance, jazz, ballet, national, Latin American or any other sort of dance I may have missed out" – she did a little chuckle – "then let me know by the weekend and I can get to work on the programme. You have to produce about three to five minutes worth of dancing, but it must be of a high standard." Mrs. Truman stressed the word *must*. "I don't know you Year Sevens too well yet, so if any of you has any particular talent, do please come along and tell me, and then we can see what you might be able to do in the show. So far, we've got tap, modern, street and ballet routines, which have been organized through the individual junior and senior clubs, but there's no reason why people shouldn't work out their own routines without any teachers involved, and then I can check them through and see if they're up to scratch." She smiled around at us all. "Anyway, have a think about it, and don't forget, let me know by the weekend."

We six didn't bother to change at the end of gym, as it was the last lesson. We just put our tracksuits on to walk back to Forest Ash.

"The dance show sounds exciting, doesn't it?" Sasha said, when we'd hardly set off.

And then the words I'd been dreading came up, as I knew they would. "Izzy, you must definitely dance in it! You'd be a natural," said Nicole. "I mean, you must have done some sort of dancing when you were younger."

"Yes, you weell be our Emerald dancer!" said Antonia, her eyes all sparkly. "You can dance for us all."

My mouth felt dry. "I...don't really want to," I said carefully. "I don't actually do...dancing any more." I didn't look round but I could just feel lots of eyes on me, including Sasha's. I thought I ought to add something more final to close the conversation completely. "It's in my past."

The moment the words were out of my mouth I regretted them, because they sounded too dramatic. There was a silence, and I had no idea how to fill it.

"Wh...*what* exactly is in your past?" asked Bryony, looking puzzled.

"Ballet." There. I'd said it.

"So, you did do ballet once...right?" said Bryony, still looking a bit confused.

It was Emily who tried to get straight to the point. "Why didn't you tell us? Don't you like it any more, Izzy?"

Yes, I love it, said the *other me*.

"No," I answered, my voice coming out a bit more firmly than I'd meant it to.

Sasha linked her arm through mine. "Well, it'll be good fun watching, anyway," she said brightly. "I wonder if it'll be in the theatre?"

No one answered and I felt embarrassed for making the atmosphere awkward, and for making Sasha feel sorry for me. I was sure she would bring up the subject later when we were on our own, but I really didn't want her to. Maybe my *no* that had come out like a bullet would make her think twice about it though.

Every evening during the week we have prep for an hour, which is just like homework except that we work in silence in a room at Forest Ash with one of the teachers supervising. Tonight it was Mrs. Pridham, our lovely housemistress, and she must have been concentrating hard on whatever she was reading, because she didn't notice how often I went into a daydream. The trouble was, the *other me* couldn't stop thinking about the dance show. I kept on going over and over Mrs. Truman's words. *So far, we've got tap, modern, street and ballet routines, which have been organized through the individual junior and senior clubs.*

I'd realized that Maria and Olivia must be members of the senior ballet club and that their group would be performing in the show. But what about the junior club? Would there be girls of my age dancing? What would it be like sitting in the audience watching them? It made me upset just thinking about it.

My prep wasn't getting done and no matter how much I tried to concentrate, I'd lost the thread and that made me restless, so in the end I put my hand up and asked if I could go to the loo. Mrs. Pridham smiled and nodded. "Yes, of course, Izzy."

I didn't really need the loo. I was just desperate to have a few moments to myself to be alone with my secret. The loos were a good place to go – nice and private, especially during prep time. I stood up straight, facing the mirrors above the sink, and checked in the full-length mirror to the side that my whole body was in alignment.

Miss Amelia was always talking about alignment. Nothing must be even a millimetre lopsided. I pulled up out of my ribs and tightened my stomach and leg muscles. I lifted my chin just the tiniest bit, then, very slowly, balancing on my turned-out left leg, I raised my right knee and unfolded my leg until my foot was just above the level of my waist, pointing out to the side. At the same time I moved my arms up above my head into what is called fifth position in ballet. I was in a full *developpé* and I hadn't wobbled on my supporting leg one single time. It felt wonderful holding that position, even though I'd still got my baggy tracky bums on. But then I heard footsteps outside in the corridor and my magic moment had to stop. So I lowered my leg and closed to first position.

By the time the door opened, I was washing my hands.

"Hi," said the Year Eleven girl who'd just come in.

"Hi," I said back. We smiled at each other in the mirror.

"You look happy."

I smiled again. "Yes..." Then I dried my hands and went out.

That moment in the toilets had made me desperate to practise for longer. It had been a good *developpé*, but I could have made it better. I was feeling a little tinge of anxiety creeping in that I hadn't raised my leg high enough. When I'd been having classes with Miss Amelia, I'd always been able to raise my leg in a *developpé* until my foot was level with my shoulder. But then by the time I'd started at Silver Spires, I'd got completely out of practice and had lost quite a bit of suppleness. That was the reason my secret life first started. I simply couldn't bear the feeling that I'd lost my flexibility, so I would go off secretly whenever I knew I wouldn't be missed and, more importantly, to a place where I didn't think anyone would be around, and steal a few minutes to practise.

At first I only did it once or twice a week, but these days I'd started to find myself snatching odd moments much more often than that, and worrying all the more in case anyone ever found out. That would be terrible. My friends would think I was so odd, especially since I'd told them I didn't like ballet any more. It was a big relief that some of my flexibility was back, but if I was honest, it wasn't only for that reason that I kept up my secret practices. It was also because the *other me* just didn't seem able to let go of ballet, even though I knew it was stupid and pointless and there was absolutely no future in it for me now.

* * *

That night I woke up with a start. I'd had a bad dream about my audition at The Royal Ballet School. I often have this dream, but it's never usually such a nightmare as it was this time. I dreamed that when I saw my reflection in the mirrors, my body wasn't my own. I'd grown into a really weird shape and when I watched myself dancing it looked terrible, like someone who had no idea what they were doing. And the panel of judges folded their arms and turned almost purple with rage as they watched me, and eventually one of them stood up and, without saying a word, he marched me out of the room. Then he turned and went back inside, shutting the door behind him. The worst part of the dream was what happened next though. Very slowly, some black letters appeared on the door and it took me a while to realize what they said, but then suddenly they were crystal clear: *KEEP OUT!*

My heart was beating really loudly as I sat up in bed and hugged the duvet around me. I was desperate to switch my light on, but I didn't want to wake up any of the others. So I sat there in the dark, shivering and going over the dream, because my mum once told me that bad dreams won't come back straight away as long as you think them through when you're properly awake and try and laugh at how silly and unreal they are. The trouble was, *my* dream felt totally real, especially the expression on the judges' faces, because I knew all the dream judges in real life. One of them was a man who worked in a newspaper kiosk back home, so what he was doing in my dream I don't know. But the other two were Miss Amelia and a man I'd seen when I'd done my actual audition.

I couldn't bear the memory of the look I'd seen on Miss Amelia's face in my dream. It was as though she hated me. And I couldn't picture her nice smiling face any more, because her horrible dream expression kept popping up instead.

In the end I found myself creeping down my ladder and opening my bottom drawer to get my pile of ballet stuff out from the very back. I wanted to get the picture of Miss Amelia from amongst all the photos, because I thought if I could actually see her face it might help get rid of the dream. I got back into bed with the pile and as no one seemed to have stirred, even with me moving around so much, I thought it might be safe to switch on my little light for a minute. No one woke up, so after a few seconds I relaxed and carefully went through the photos until I came to the one of Miss Amelia. I was expecting to feel a big relief sweep over me at the sight of her face, but in fact I just felt horribly sad, as usual, about how my dancing had not been as good as either of us had hoped.

I turned to the next photo in the pile. It was a picture of me dancing in the last show I'd done with Miss Amelia. I'd had the main part, and the photo showed me holding an *arabesque*, which is when you balance on one leg and extend the other leg up high behind you, without turning your hips sideways, but making sure your leg is turned out right down to the end of your foot. Your back tilts forwards a bit, but not too much, and you have to hold the balance and keep your legs stretched but your arms soft, as Miss Amelia used to say.

Seeing the photo now made me want to get back out of bed, stand in the middle of the dorm and try an *arabesque* right there and then, but obviously I couldn't do that because if one of the others woke up and saw me there they'd get the shock of their lives. But I wasn't ready to go back to sleep yet, so I went through my ballet autograph book, turning the pages slowly because I loved comparing all the signatures.

I was back in my other world, completely forgetting that it was the middle of the night and I should really be asleep. I had a stunning photo of

Jaimie Tapper from The Royal Ballet that I'd cut out of a ballet magazine, and I'd also got her autograph when Mum had taken me to see her dancing in the ballet *Coppélia*. I think that was the precise time when I'd vowed to myself that ballet was definitely the only career I ever, ever wanted for myself when I was older. I started imagining the whole story of that particular ballet. In my imagination, I was right in the middle of the bit where Swanilda creeps into Doctor Coppelius's house and stares in shock at all the life-size clockwork dolls, when I nearly jumped out of my skin at the sound of Sasha's voice.

"What are you doing, Izzy?"

"I…nothing," I whispered into the gloom.

She was leaning on one elbow and squinting at me from her bed, which is close to mine. "What are you looking at? Why are you awake?"

I was worried that the others might wake up at the sound of Sasha's voice, because she wasn't speaking very quietly.

"I had a bad dream," I whispered. "I'm fine now, honestly. Go back to sleep, Sash."

But she was getting out of her bed. "It's okay, I'm awake now," she said, a bit more softly this time. She climbed down her ladder and up mine, while I tried to quickly stuff my ballet photos and things under my duvet, just keeping hold of a few. But then I realized Sasha was about to sit on top of where I'd hidden everything, so I whipped the pile out and put it under the pillow just in time.

"But what *are* you doing, Izzy?"

I spoke in the softest whisper. "Just looking at these pictures... They're nothing much. It's just that I haven't got a good book and I wanted to make my eyes tired, so then I might be able to get back to sleep."

Sasha had squashed in beside me, so we were both sitting up with our legs under the duvet. She took the small pile of photos and cuttings and things I was holding and I tried not to tense up too obviously. I wasn't even sure which ones they were, because I'd had to act so quickly.

Her voice when she spoke was just as quiet as mine had been. "This is a lovely picture, Whizz. Is it a famous ballerina?"

I nodded and whispered back, "It's Darcey Bussell. She's retired now."

"Retired? Was this picture taken years ago then? Because she looks really young."

"No, ballet dancers retire in their thirties usually. Darcey was actually forty, I think. That's old for a ballerina."

Sasha was looking at me. "You know an awful lot about ballet, Izzy, don't you?"

I nodded and shrugged. The *other me* wanted to carry on talking and talking like this with my best friend about my favourite subject, but the *new me* knew I must be careful not to. "I used to be really interested in it."

There was a pause, then she looked at the next picture. "Who's this?"

"It's Marie Rambert, the founder of the Ballet Rambert, that's called Rambert Dance Company now."

Sasha brought the photo closer to her face. "She looks nice. Kind."

I nodded.

"Where's the rest of the stuff? You had loads more a moment ago."

My heart thudded. I couldn't lie to Sasha, partly because she'd never believe me if she'd already seen the pile I was holding, but also simply because I couldn't lie to my best friend.

I reached under my pillow and felt relieved that there was so little light that she wouldn't be able to tell that I'd gone a bit red. "I...I put them under here so they wouldn't get squashed or anything."

She took the programmes and other cuttings and

things carefully out of my hands and laid them on the duvet in front of her. "Yes, they must be really precious."

I didn't say anything.

She was engrossed in slowly going through the pile, one thing at a time. "Are these your most treasured possessions?" she asked.

Sasha was getting too close to the truth. "No... not really."

She suddenly broke off what she was doing and looked me straight in the eyes. I tried not to appear flustered but it wasn't easy, because any moment now she was going to get to the photo of me dancing in that final show before I'd given up Miss Amelia's classes. And I absolutely didn't want her to see that one. I just knew that if she did, it would set off loads of questions that I wouldn't be able to answer.

"I'm really tired now, Sash," I tried. "Shall we try to get back to sleep? Sorry I woke you up."

She started to leaf through the pile really quickly then. "It wasn't your fault. I think I just happened to wake up of my own accord, and then I saw your light."

I tried not to sound too urgent. "It's quarter past two, Sash."

And then the photo of me was suddenly at the top and Sasha stared at it and gasped. "Oh Izzy, is this you? Wow! You look amazing!"

I could feel a tightness blocking my throat, the kind of tightness you get when you're going to cry, and I didn't trust myself to speak.

"Izzy...?"

"Mmm."

"Why don't you like talking about ballet?"

I bit my lip, then swallowed and spoke as casually as I could. "I don't know. It's just that I've given it up, that's all."

Sasha looked at me carefully and I shrugged and smiled. "Come on. We're going to be yawning all through lessons tomorrow!"

It had taken every bit of energy I had to sound so unconcerned. But it worked, because Sasha nodded. "Yes, you're right."

Then she crept down the ladder. I followed her so I could put my stuff away. Perhaps if there wasn't a single trace of it left in the morning, I could pretend that our ballet talk never happened.

Chapter Three

Weekends at Silver Spires are great because there are always outings and shopping trips, and the chance to watch DVDs or to go swimming or just hang out with your friends. We have lessons till lunchtime on Saturday and then we're free. Some weekends there are really great activities, like kite flying and abseiling, and those are the kinds of things that Bryony always chooses to do because she's the most tomboyish and adventurous of us all. There are theatre trips occasionally too, and outings to the cinema or to play tenpin bowling or go ice skating. Antonia, Nicole, Sasha and I often want to stick together and do the same things, and it's really nice to be part of such a lovely group. Then there's Emily. Her big passion is riding. She goes to the local stables every Saturday afternoon and comes back all muddy and happy.

On the Saturday afternoon after we heard from Mrs. Truman about the dance show, Emily had gone riding and Bryony had joined a big party of girls who were hiking. Nicole and Antonia were in the dorm watching a DVD of an Italian film with subtitles on Antonia's laptop, and Sasha had gone to the art block to help paint the scenery for a play that was going to be performed at the end of term. She'd tried to persuade me to go too, but I'd been looking out for the chance to secretly practise ballet on my own and this seemed like the perfect opportunity. I'd said I'd join her a bit later after I'd done a few e-mails.

I only planned to send one e-mail, to Mum and Dad, filling them in with all my news, but there was an e-mail from Max in my inbox, which surprised me because he'd never e-mailed me before. I read it quickly and found myself gasping with shock.

Hey Iz,

How's life at SS? Hope you're still having fun and getting to know more people.

Got some sad news I'm afraid. Claire and I have split up. We had a massive argument and just don't seem to be able to resolve it, so in the end I told her I didn't want to see her any more. I'm sure I've done the right thing, even though I'm missing her like mad. Anyway, just wanted to let you know because she won't be around during the hols when you're home at Christmas. I'm off out with Pete in a mo, so see ya soon!

Holly sends her love.

And love from me too, bro Max

I hated the thought of Christmas without Claire being around some of the time, because for one thing I'd already decided on a present for her, but also it just wouldn't be the same having Max moping around on his own. It didn't seem right somehow. I quickly replied to him, telling him I was really sorry they'd split up, especially if he was still missing her, but I didn't ask what the argument was about and I didn't try to persuade him to change his mind because Max gets irritated quite quickly if he thinks people are sticking their noses into his business. So I just concentrated on talking about life at Silver Spires, and how Emily keeps us all in stitches without even meaning to be funny, and how Matron is trying to learn Italian and Antonia has to hide her giggles whenever Matron says something because apparently her accent is really over the top.

When I'd sent the e-mail, I went down to the laundry room in the basement. People don't go in there much on Saturdays. It's where we put all our stuff to be washed. There are big drums for different types of washing, all labelled *DARK SCHOOL UNIFORM, LIGHT SCHOOL UNIFORM,* etc. Then there's a drying room to the side of the laundry room where our clothes are stacked in piles for us to collect, and there's a door that leads out of that room into a room that just seems to be spare. You'd hardly notice the door, because it's tucked around a corner. And anyway, there'd be no reason for anyone to go into the spare room, because it's completely empty apart from a few old chairs.

I was wearing a T-shirt and my tracky bums and trainers, and carrying my iPod, and as soon as I pushed the door to the little room open I felt the jitters that I always get when I'm about to have some precious moments to myself. But at the same time I was worried that I shouldn't be doing this. It always seems too secretive, as though I'm doing something wrong.

When I get these confused thoughts I have to shake them away or I'll drive myself mad. So that's what I did as I kicked off my shoes and pulled a chair from the wall. The back of the chair was the perfect height for a *barre*. Next I found the music that I use for *barre* work on my iPod, and placed my hand on the chair, waiting for Miss Amelia's voice to come to me. Usually it's easy to imagine her correcting my arm position or my hips or my feet, but today I didn't hear anything apart from the beat of the music. It was as though, on this very day, I'd finally moved too far away from her, and I'd have to forget about my old classes and learn to correct *myself* in future. It was quite frightening when I realized that, but I was ready for hard work, so I began.

I wished there'd been enough time to spend a whole hour doing nothing but *barre* work, but I knew I ought to get over to the art block before too long or Sasha would wonder what had become of me, and there was so much more ballet I wanted to do first. So I changed the track on my iPod, moved to the centre of the room and started my *adage*, which is a series of slow, expressive exercises for the arms. I only allowed myself five minutes on this section. Then I did some jumps and made up a few little routines by putting a set of steps together, which gave me the feeling I was dancing properly.

Actually it wasn't properly at all, because the room is so small, but I used every square centimetre of the floor.

It was horrible having to finish my secret class, but I knew it was time I was getting over to the art block, so I put my trainers on and went back into the drying room. I kept my iPod on though, because at least the music allowed me to stay in my secret world for a little while longer.

I was about to go through to the laundry room when my eye fell on someone's pink ballet tights. I stared at them for a few seconds and felt shocked because a wave of jealousy had come over me. Maybe these were Olivia's or Maria's tights. Or were there other girls at Forest Ash who did ballet? I'd no idea. I went closer and touched the pale pink stretchy material that was so familiar. Then I realized there were actually two pairs, and also two pairs of leg warmers lying on the shelf beside them.

Before I knew it I was staring around the whole room, looking to see if there were any leotards anywhere, but there weren't. Then my mind flitted back to Olivia and Maria. They were probably practising their dance at this very moment. I so envied them. They would be in a proper dance studio with a lovely sprung floor and *barres* and music, while I'd been stuck in a bare little room with a dirty floor. I looked at the floor of this drying room. It was actually cleaner than the floor in the room I'd just been in, but it was boiling hot in here and very noisy. I think some kind of machine was swooshing away or maybe it was just water in the pipes. The shelves were the right height for a *barre* though, and before I knew it, I'd reached out and placed my hand on one of them, just to see what it felt like. And then of course, I had to try out some steps...

"Hey, Izzy, what are you doing?"

My stomach seemed to yo-yo for a second and I turned to see Emily standing there. Her red hair was dripping wet and she was carrying a plastic bag that looked as though it was full of clothes.

"Nothing much." I yanked the earphones out of my ears. "Did you have a good ride?" I quickly changed the subject. "You're back early, aren't you?"

"It was totally brilliant!" she said. "I got soaked. Look." She opened her bag. "Feel that."

"Oh wow!" I said, my hand touching the wet sweatshirt. "I didn't even know it was raining!" The moment the words were out of my mouth I could have kicked myself.

"You didn't even know! But it's been raining for ages! Listen."

I suddenly realized that the noise I'd been hearing that I thought was the pipes or some kind of machine whirring away was actually the rain hammering against the building. I'd been so caught up in my world of ballet that I hadn't noticed the downpour outside.

Emily was frowning at me. "So what are you doing down here if you're not drying your clothes out like me?"

My face was hotter than ever and I was sure I must have gone red. What could I say? I didn't even have any laundry to collect. "I...I thought I'd still got my jeans to pick up but then I remembered I already picked them up yesterday."

Emily wasn't really listening, thank goodness. She'd dropped her bag of clothes and was standing in the middle of the room. But my relief soon turned to shock. "Show me those ballet steps you were doing. You looked so cool, Iz."

I'd really thought I'd got away with it, but now it looked as though Emily had been paying more attention to me than I'd thought.

"I...can't remember what I did."

"Do anything then. You're totally talented, Izzy!

None of us get why you don't go to junior ballet club."

I had to be firm about this so we could drop the subject. "I told you, I don't do ballet any more. I was just mucking about."

But Emily was gripping the shelf with her right hand. "Is this right, Izzy?" She tried to turn her feet into first position, but it made her bottom stick out. So then she arched her back, which made her stomach push forwards. There was no way I could correct her. I wouldn't know where to start. "I can't even stand in the proper position!" she wailed. "Just show me how to stand, Iz. Go on!"

I decided it would be best to get it over with, so I prepared in first position with my arm to the side, feeling really self-conscious, especially when I saw that Emily was watching me intently.

"Don't bother to teach me," she suddenly said in a voice of sighs that I'd never heard her use before. "There's no way in a trillion years that I'd be able to look like you." Then she laughed. "I'll just stick to horse riding, I think."

I laughed too, and tried to change the conversation quickly. "Do you want to come over to the art block with me? I was just going to help Sasha paint scenery for the play."

"No, it's okay. My mum sent me the latest issue of my horsey magazine and I want to read it from cover to cover once I've hung this wet stuff up."

"Okay, see you later, then."

"Yeah, see ya!"

So off I went. But my footsteps felt heavy as I made my way to the art block. My secret world had been invaded and I wasn't comfortable with that.

In one way it was a good thing it had been Emily and not one of the others who'd caught me doing ballet. Emily is the most scatty of us all, in a lovely way, and she's not that interested in anything except horses and gardening and farming. There was quite a good chance that she'd simply forget about seeing me in the drying room and never mention it to the others.

I felt happier by the time I reached the art block. But not completely happy. There was still the voice of the *other me*, gabbling urgently to the *new me*...

Even if Emily doesn't say anything, someone will one day, because you're not going to stop practising ballet. Not ever. You love it too much.

Chapter Four

On Sunday evening we went to the common room to play our favourite game, Uno. But we'd only just dealt out the cards for the first round when Maria and Olivia came crashing in, both out of breath. They were wearing ballet tights with leg warmers, and tracksuit tops, and both moved like dancers, despite their trainers. Even when they flopped down on one of the sofas, it was a graceful movement and I could tell they were ballet trained. I knew I wasn't the only one of my friends to think so either, because Emily was supposed to be playing the first card, only she was too busy staring at Maria and Olivia.

"Go on, Emily," I said quietly, worrying like mad in case she made a connection between Maria and Olivia being dancers, and me, and came out with something about my ballet exercises in the drying room. I'd spent the rest of the day before feeling tense, waiting for Emily to bring it up, but when bedtime arrived and she hadn't said a word, I'd begun to relax. I'd hardly given it a thought today, but now suddenly I was having to worry all over again.

"Oh yes!" said Emily, her eyes jerking back to the game. She frowned at her cards as if she was forcing herself to concentrate.

But then came Maria's dramatic voice: "I'm completely exhausted, aren't you, Liv?"

I noticed Bryony give Emily a look as if to say, *Those two really fancy themselves, don't they?* but Emily didn't notice. She was back to staring at the two older girls and I so wished she'd stop so we could just get on with the game. But the others seemed as mesmerized by Maria and Olivia as Emily was. There was something about their presence that made you want to look at them. Maria had tucked her feet underneath her and was resting her arm in a graceful way on the back of the sofa.

Olivia was leaning forwards with a completely straight back, taking off her trainers. Then she pulled off her socks and started massaging her toes. "I don't know what we're going to do without Abi, you know."

There were some Year Nines in the common room. They'd looked as though they were absolutely glued to something on telly, but the moment they realized who was talking, they seemed to lose interest in what they were watching, as one by one they turned their attention to Olivia and Maria.

"Have you two just been to rehearsal?" asked a girl called Alice, brightly.

Olivia drew a deep breath and when she spoke her voice sounded low and serious. "Yes, and we've got a big problem."

"Why? What's up?" asked another one of the Year Nines.

"Abi's done something to her leg," said Maria.

There were gasps from the Year Nines. "She's your best dancer, isn't she?" said someone else.

I saw Olivia kind of flinch. "She's got the biggest part, if that's what you mean," she answered in a bit of a snap.

"And now we're stuck not knowing whether someone else ought to take over her role in case the hamstring injury is serious and long term, or whether to just carry on as we are and hope she gets better in time," Maria explained. "But I can't tell you what a hard dance it is and it's practically impossible with one person missing."

"Who's Abi?" Emily suddenly piped up.

Maria and Olivia glanced across at our table for no more than a second, then as soon as they saw we were a bunch of Year Sevens, turned straight back to the Year Nines without even bothering to answer.

Alice gave Emily an answer though. "Abi is a brilliant ballet dancer in Year Ten. She's in Oakley House."

Olivia sighed loudly. "I'm just going to have to learn Abi's part as well as my own," she said.

"Or I could learn it, if you want," said Maria.

"No, it's okay, I'll learn it," said Olivia, quickly. Then she got up and went across to the far side of the common room, walking with her feet turned right out. I thought she looked a bit silly and instantly felt anxious in case I looked that silly when I walked. When you've done a lot of ballet training you can't help walking with your feet turned out a bit, but not as much as Olivia's.

I think every single pair of eyes in the common room was on Olivia as she took her tracksuit top off and dropped it on the floor. She was wearing a tight ballet top underneath, and I had to admit her arms and shoulders looked really strong and supple. It seemed like she knew she was the centre of attention and was showing off how flexible she was as she dropped in slow motion into the splits, with her right leg in front, then turned and shifted her weight so she was in the sideways splits.

"Oh wow! You're so supple, Olivia. That's amazing!" said a girl called Dee.

And as the other Year Nines all agreed in murmurs, I noticed they'd now paused the DVD they were watching.

The look in Maria's eyes changed and I realized she was jealous. I don't think she liked everyone watching Olivia, and it suddenly seemed odd that the two girls acted like such friends and yet they weren't really.

Olivia moved smoothly into a shape on her stomach, then rolled over gracefully and sat up. "This is where we help Abi up, isn't it?" she said to Maria, as though they were practising all on their own somewhere, instead of in a crowded common room full of admiring girls. I looked round my friends and saw that Bryony was restless. Our eyes met and she grinned at me, then shook her head slightly as if to say, *What a show-off!* I grinned back, feeling relieved that I wasn't the only one to think that. But the others were still staring in admiration as Maria went across and helped Olivia to her feet, then broke into a sequence of *pas de bourrées, chassés* and *pirouettes*. It wasn't a difficult combination of steps but it looked impressive and the Year Nines broke into applause.

Olivia ignored them and began to unfold her leg into a *developpé* and Maria pouted. "It's not fair! Why do I have to be the one to use my left leg for that bit?"

"For the balance of the dance, of course," said Olivia.

"But why can't *you* do the left-legged *developpé* and I'll do the right-legged one? It's much easier."

Olivia waved her hand dismissively. "Whatever. I'm equally supple on both sides."

I suddenly felt desperate to get out of this room. There was something stifling me and it wasn't just the horrible rivalry between the two girls. It was the fact they were doing ballet right in front of me. I don't know why, but a picture of Mum flashed through my mind. It was a time when she'd given up chocolate for Lent and my brother was teasing her by eating some Belgian chocolates that Claire had bought him, right in front of Mum. At first Mum had just laughed, but I'll never forget the envious look on her face as she watched Max eating more and more of them and talking with his mouth full about how delicious they were.

"I usually think ballet's quite boring, but when I watch you two, I wish I'd learned it myself," said Dee, bringing me back to the here and now. "I can't wait to see the show."

"The show will be cool. We've got a great routine in the jazz dance club," said a really nice girl called Meg.

Dee nodded hard. "I remember the jazz group last year. They were brilliant."

"Well, I saw some Year Eights practising a tap routine in the sports hall yesterday," said Alice. "And I tell you, it looked amazing!"

"At least the juniors are doing *something*!" said Olivia, moving her arms through an *adage* that I recognized from an exam I'd done.

"You're so graceful, Olivia," said Dee.

Olivia didn't reply, but I could tell from her face that she was pleased.

"Aren't the juniors doing very much in the show then?" Emily asked.

It was Meg who replied. "Yes, there are a few doing tap and pop, but I think Olivia means there's no one doing ballet."

My heart thudded.

"The junior ballet club hasn't got any talent at all," said Maria, pulling a face. "I watched them last week. Miss Morgan told me afterwards that it might have to fold because people keep dropping out and no one seems really committed."

"Yeah, but it's not really to do with being committed," said Meg, looking a bit scared to be speaking out against Maria. "I was in that club last year, and we performed in the show and everyone in the audience seemed a bit bored. It wasn't fair, because it's so hard to make ballet look good. I mean it's miles easier with jazz and disco and stuff."

"Exactly," said Olivia. "That's 'cos ballet is way more difficult than any other sort of dance, so you have to work harder at it. And quite honestly, unless you've done loads of training before you come to Silver Spires, like right up to grade five or something, you're not going to be able to carry off a performance."

"Izzy's great at ballet!" Emily suddenly said. And I felt as though someone had poured ice cubes down my spine. I just froze.

Then one of the Year Nines looked over at our table and asked which of us was Izzy, and Emily got up and pointed at me. I could have died. Olivia and Maria shot me the quickest glance in the world as they carried straight on with what they were doing.

Out of the corner of my eye, I saw Sasha and Emily exchange a look. I couldn't see Sasha's face, but Emily immediately turned her palms up innocently. "What?" she said indignantly. "She *is* good. I've seen her. I know!"

"No, I'm not," I said quietly. It sounded pathetic, but I didn't know what else to say.

"Let's get on with the game!" said Sasha. "Come on, Emily. It's you to start."

And as if she'd issued a command, the frozen picture on the TV screen sprang back into life for a few seconds, before someone switched it off altogether and the Year Nine girls trooped out, chatting.

"We'll watch it another time, yeah?"

"Yes, I've forgotten what was going on now."

"The dance show's going to be great!"

"I know. I can't wait!"

And a moment later Olivia put her socks and shoes back on and she and Maria left the common room too, almost as though there was no point practising in there when there was only a bunch of Year Sevens watching them.

In one way it was a relief when everyone had gone out, but my whole body was still tense, and with Emily's next words I felt as though I was standing at the very edge of a cliff.

"Why don't you go to junior ballet club, Iz?" She laid her cards down on the table suddenly. "I mean, you heard what they said about how it might have to fold. I bet you'd easily be the best. In fact, I reckon you could even be better than Maria and Olivia, actually!"

Emily leaned back in her chair and folded her arms, and I bit my lip and squirmed around in my own chair, not knowing what to say.

Sasha put her arm round me. "Leave her alone, Emily."

"Sasha's right, she obviously doesn't want to talk about it, so let's just get on with the game," Bryony added.

I wanted to say thank you, but even those two little words would have drawn the attention back to me, so I sat there stiffly and we carried on playing. But it was ages before we truly got back into the game. And when we did, I was rubbish. I kept on laying the wrong cards because of all the thoughts that were whizzing through my mind. All the things I wished I could say to try and explain myself...

I can't go to junior ballet club. Can I?

No. What would be the point when I'm never going to be a ballet dancer. It would just be too painful. I'd have to look in the mirrors and face my failure.

Chapter Five

The following Wednesday, Sasha and I went to gym club and for a whole hour we had a brilliant time. The session was all about flight. We had to work on the benches and springboards using three jump shapes called tuck, pike and straddle, and then we got to do the jumps off the bigger pieces of apparatus, which was scary but amazing.

Every so often I thought, *What if I fall awkwardly or twist my ankle or something? That would be terrible for my ballet.* But then I reminded myself sternly that it doesn't matter about that. I don't do ballet any more. Well, not properly. Just on my own, which doesn't count. At least…I don't think it does.

At the end of the club, Sasha went to ask Mrs. Truman if she could go through something with her, and I hung around waiting for her. It seemed like she really wanted to improve her vaults, as she was concentrating hard on everything Mrs. Truman said and trying to make her technique better. She tried one particular vault out two or three times.

By the time Mrs. Truman had finished helping Sasha, everyone else had gone, and even Mrs. Truman herself got a shock when she saw the time. "Oh my goodness. I'd better get myself organized!" And she rushed out of the hall, leaving me and Sasha alone.

I started to walk towards the changing room, but Sasha's voice stopped me. She was still in her serious mode. "Izzy?"

"Yes?"

"Now that there's only you and me here, can you just show me one little ballet step?" She broke into a gabble and I suddenly realized she was nervous about how I might react. "I don't mind what step it is. Just anything. Or maybe do what you showed Emily. She said you held onto the shelf and started in first position…?"

I realized so much in that moment. Firstly, it sounded from what Sasha had said – *Now that there's only you and me here* – like she may have deliberately kept Mrs. Truman talking about gym by pretending she wanted to know something, when all she was really doing was killing time till the rest of the girls had gone, so she and I could be on our own. And secondly, Sasha and Emily must have talked to each other about me and my ballet.

And yet I wasn't cross. And even more surprising, I wasn't upset that my private world had been invaded again. I think it was because of being in the sports hall. The big empty space was just so tempting that my feet tingled and the tingles ran up my legs and spread out all over my body. I told myself one little step or two would be all right, especially as it was just me and my best friend this time. So I slowly stepped into the preparation position for one of the grade six set variations that I really loved, and I was aware of Sasha shuffling quickly backwards as though to give me space.

But then a second later I forgot about her completely because the familiar music for that variation came swirling into my head and I was beginning to move into an *arabesque*, then a *port de bras* and then something faster – some *sissonnes*.

And that was the moment when the music was suddenly spoiled by the noise of a squeaky door, and I stopped abruptly, and stood there feeling shaky and strange.

"Izzy! That was lovely." Mrs. Truman was rushing over to the mats. "I've got senior gym club in here now, but you'll have to show me some more ballet in the next PE lesson?" She'd raised her voice as though it was a question and now she was looking at me waiting for an answer. So was Sasha.

I stood there silently, like an idiot.

"You're not in junior ballet club, are you?" Mrs. Truman carried on. "I'll have a word with Miss Morgan. I know she's wanting to boost the numbers of girls doing ballet at the junior end of the school."

"I'm...not really all that interested."

Mrs. Truman had been dragging mats about, but she stopped and looked at me carefully, her head tipped on one side. "You seem to have a natural talent, Izzy. It would be a shame to let it go."

I was suddenly aware of Sasha out of the corner of my eye. She was nodding. "Yes, Izzy's definitely really talented," she said, sounding a bit breathless and I saw that her cheeks had gone pink.

Mrs. Truman smiled at Sasha. "Absolutely!"

Then she turned to me. "I'll get Miss Morgan to size you up." I felt my stomach knotting. I hated those words.

But then the conversation came to an abrupt halt, thank goodness, because some seniors had come into the hall and one of them had broken into cartwheels.

"Not without getting warmed up, Natalie!" Mrs. Truman called out, sounding strict. She tutted a bit and pretended to be crosser than she was, and I felt relieved that something was happening to take the attention away from me. Without wasting a second, I hurried to the door and Sasha immediately rushed to join me.

An awkwardness hung between us once we were outside, just like the one when we'd been in the common room with Maria and Olivia and the Year Nines.

It was Sasha who broke the silence, still sounding nervous. "I didn't know Mrs. Truman was coming back, Whizz, honestly," she said.

"It's okay." It was hard to know what else to say. "I didn't really mind," I went on, trying to sound normal. "I just don't want to join ballet club, that's all, and I don't like it when people try to persuade me to."

That was the most I'd ever said on the subject and I could see from Sasha's wide eyes that she was really interested and curious.

"Why not?" she asked simply.

I suddenly thought there might be a way I could explain myself. A way that Sasha would understand. "Because ballet's different from lots of other subjects. It's either something you do..." I hesitated to say the next three words because they were giving away too much of my private world. I spoke them softly and quickly to try and cover them up a bit. "...*for the future*...or otherwise it's something you don't do at all." Sasha's eyes were enormous by then and I just wanted to drop the whole conversation. "That's how I think about it, anyway," I said, trying to lighten my voice. "It's no big deal."

Those last four words must have come out with a harder edge than I'd meant, because Sasha opened her mouth as though she was about to say something, but quickly closed it again. And we walked in silence for a few steps until some birds started to sing and I felt a sudden rush of magic.

"Listen!" I said, stopping in my tracks. "Birds singing when it's practically dark! That's unusual isn't it?"

We stood there completely motionless, listening

to two little birds tweeting away, and to me it felt like a bond between us. I think Sasha had the same thought, because she broke into a big smile. "It's lovely here, isn't it, Iz? We're so lucky, aren't we?"

I nodded. And we walked on chattering about the different boarding houses and how pleased we were to be in Forest Ash. And I *did* feel lucky, because it was just as though the ballet conversation had been sealed over and we were back to normal again.

Chapter Six

The next day I woke up with the feeling that it was going to be a good day. Just before I'd gone to sleep last night, I'd thought through what had happened in the sports hall and decided that I was pleased Sasha had seen me dancing now and heard me telling Mrs. Truman that I wasn't interested in joining the ballet club. And I remembered again how she'd stopped Emily from talking about ballet in front of me too. I was so lucky to have Sasha as a best friend. Now I'd told her why I didn't like talking about ballet, I had the feeling that she wouldn't ask again, and also that she'd try and protect me from anyone else nagging me to do something I didn't want to do.

At morning break, Nicole wanted to show us how much Italian she'd learned. She and Antonia actually had a conversation in Italian. Antonia was pretending to be the shopkeeper and Nicole was buying all sorts of things and talking about the weather. It was really impressive and the rest of us clapped like mad at the end. Then the two of them started trying to teach *us* how to speak the language, but we couldn't pronounce the words properly, which made Antonia fall about laughing and say we were worse than Matron. Her laughter was infectious and before long we were all practically in hysterics.

Then I got a text from Max and read it quickly.

Ta 4 e-mail. Still missin C.

Part from that

all good. U ok?

I felt really proud to be the person Max was confiding in about missing Claire. I mean I knew I probably wasn't the only one, but I felt quite grown-up and happy, especially because he seemed to be keeping in touch more now than when I first joined Silver Spires.

"It's from my brother," I said quietly to Sasha. "He says he's still missing Claire."

"Poor Max," said Sasha.

"Why? What's poor about him?" asked Emily, tuning in.

"He's broken up with his girlfriend, but he's missing her," I explained quickly.

"He ought to phone her up and get back with her then," said Emily, turning her palms up as though it was obvious.

"It's not as simple as that, Ems!" said Bryony, rolling her eyes. "She might have got someone else."

"Eef she has someone else, she can domp heem!" said Antonia.

"Dump!" we all chorused, which set off another bout of hysterics.

It was geography after break, with Mr. Pattle, who's one of the strictest teachers in the school. We had a terrible time keeping our giggles inside, because we'd got ourselves in the mood for laughter and just didn't seem able to stop.

"Bryony Price, can you tell us what's amusing you this morning?" He raised his eyebrows. "I'm sure the whole class would like to know."

I was glad he'd asked Bryony. She's the bravest and toughest of us all and I knew she'd be able to stand up to Mr. Pattle without losing face.

"Yes, certainly, Mr. Pattle. I'm very sorry if we were being disruptive," she said. We all knew that she was being over-the-top polite on purpose to make fun of Mr. Pattle, which was a clever thing to do because he couldn't tell her off for being too polite. "My friends and I were laughing at ourselves for our pathetic attempts at speaking Italian during break." She smiled at him and shrugged her shoulders apologetically. "And you know what it's like when you just can't stop laughing?"

Now she was really making fun of him, because I don't suppose Mr. Pattle had any idea what that was like. I couldn't imagine he ever laughed at anything.

"Yes, well…" He looked so uncomfortable standing there now. I couldn't believe how flustered he was, and I almost felt sorry for him, except that what happened next killed every last trace of laughter that might have been lingering inside me.

Miss Morgan had come into the room. "I'm sorry to interrupt, Mr. Pattle, but could I borrow Izzy Carter for a few minutes?"

Mr. Pattle looked hugely relieved at the distraction and nodded at me to go. I saw Sasha's hand fly to her mouth and I knew she was worried about how I'd react to the dance mistress wanting to speak to me. My legs shook as I got up and looked at Miss Morgan. Then as her eyes met mine, I realized that she didn't have a clue who I was. She was just following up on what Mrs. Truman had told her.

My heart thudded as we walked down the corridor together. And I felt as though my feet were thudding too, because Miss Morgan was so tiny and graceful, walking beside me in her pink footless tights and black swirly dance skirt and tight white top with a thin green wrap-over. On her feet she wore ballet-teaching shoes with the tiniest of heels on them. She reminded me of Miss Amelia, and I knew it was a massive coincidence but I thought that even her perfume was the same, because I was taken right back to Miss Amelia's studio and all the classes I'd had there over the years.

"I'm sorry I had to interrupt you in your lesson, Izzy, but this is the only time I have available today and Mrs. Truman felt that I really ought to be getting you to join the junior ballet club. Only, I understand you're not very keen. Is that right?"

I nodded and tried to speak. My words came out in a small thin voice. "I've given up ballet. I found... I wasn't right for it..."

Miss Morgan was nodding. "Right..." But she

didn't sound as though she believed me.

"Wh...where are we going?"

"To the studio. I'd just like to see what you can do. You know we've got the dance show coming up, and we're a bit thin on the ground for juniors in general, but especially in ballet."

We came to the sports complex and my heart thudded as we walked past the sports hall and the small hall beside it and into the dance studio. Miss Morgan pressed four switches all at once, and the overhead lights flickered briefly, then shot bright white light into every corner of the room. I stared in amazement and felt my knees turn to jelly. No matter how much I'd taken in about this room before, it felt so different today. The baby grand piano and the rosin tray, which is for dancers to dip their pointe shoes into to help them grip the floor when they dance on the ends of their toes, took me right back to Miss Amelia's studio.

"I've got a few spare pairs of ballet shoes here, Izzy. What size are you?"

This was all going too quickly. I didn't feel as though I could say no, and yet with every fibre in my body I wanted to rush out of this studio. This was nothing like dancing on my own in secret. There was no safety here. I could see myself in every mirror, just like I had done at The Royal Ballet School audition.

My insides were turning to jelly and Miss Morgan was waiting for my reply. "Er…size four." *Please don't let her have any fours.*

"Here we are. I know it will feel a bit weird when you're in uniform instead of dancing in a leotard and tights, but I just want to get an idea."

No she didn't. She wanted to size me up. That was the phrase Mrs. Truman had used. That's what everyone wanted to do in the world of ballet. And if you weren't exactly the right fit, you were rejected. I felt as though I should be explaining to Miss Morgan that I'd already been rejected so there was no point in sizing me up a second time. And as I had that thought, it was as though the strength went out of my legs. I was shaky before, but now I was weak as well. My fingers fumbled with the ballet shoes. They weren't my own. They weren't comfortable. Did they belong to one of the seniors who'd grown out of them?

"Right, just do me a few steps like you did in the sports hall. I don't mind what, but nothing too stretchy as we don't have time for a warm-up."

Everything stiffened up as I looked at myself in the mirrors. This was so like The Royal Ballet studio where I'd auditioned that it wouldn't have surprised me if the panel of judges suddenly appeared. And as I had that thought, a picture of Miss Amelia's horrible face from my dream flashed through my mind.

"Right, off you go, Izzy." I saw Miss Morgan glance at her watch and I knew she was getting impatient, but my body just didn't seem to be able to move. I stared at the sprung floor and tried to get the feeling back that I'd had in the sports hall with Sasha. Only it wouldn't come.

"Er...I'm not really sure what..."

"Any step that you're used to, Izzy."

I couldn't put it off any longer, so I forced my arms into a preparation position, feeling how stiff they were and hating the sight of myself in the mirror. Maybe it would be better if I couldn't see myself. But there was no escape from the mirrors unless I looked down. I knew I couldn't look down though. That would completely spoil the alignment. I'd just have to get on with it quickly and then I could go. So I tried to do what I'd done in the sports hall, only it didn't work. I was too nervous and shaky and wasn't warmed up like I had been after gym club.

Miss Morgan was staring at me just like those

judges had done at The Royal Ballet School. I nearly tripped over my right foot with my left one, which I'd never, ever done before. I felt a complete fool and I stopped and said, "There," because I couldn't think what else to say.

"Oh...right!" Miss Morgan looked a bit surprised. "Do you want to try something else?"

I shook my head. What was the point?

Miss Morgan didn't try to persuade me. No wonder. She was a proper dancer. She would be able to recognize talent if she saw it. Not like Mrs. Truman. Mrs. Truman was only a PE teacher. She didn't realize I wasn't any good really.

I went back to geography on my own, because Miss Morgan had to rush off in the opposite direction. I was pleased that she wouldn't be walking along the corridor beside me, because what would we find to talk about? My shoulders slumped forwards as I walked and I dreaded going back into geography. Sasha would raise her eyebrows at me and so would the others.

And of course, that was exactly what happened. "What did she say?" whispered Sasha as I took my place next to her.

I shrugged and shook my head, which might have meant, *I'll tell you afterwards because Mr. Pattle's looking,* or it might have meant, *She didn't say anything.*

It was only a single period of geography, so the bell went in no time at all and we all trooped out. The moment we were in the corridor, all my friends crowded round me.

"What did Miss Morgan want?" asked Nicole.

"Did you show her what you could do?" asked Sasha.

"I bet she thought you were brilliant, didn't she?" said Emily.

"Are you going to join the ballet club now?" Antonia wanted to know.

Only Bryony stayed quiet, but I could tell she was interested in what I was going to say.

It was Emily's question that had stood out for me. I could answer that one easily, because I could still recall the look on Miss Morgan's face when I'd stopped and said, *There.* She'd seemed so surprised, and I imagined her talking to Mrs. Truman later: *That girl, Izzy Carter, I'm afraid I don't see any talent there. She'll never make it as a professional dancer.*

"I don't think Miss Morgan thought I was much good actually." I'd tried to sound as though I didn't really care one way or the other, but they were all looking pityingly at me, so I must have sounded a bit sorry for myself. "Anyway, I'm not joining the club, so it makes no difference what she thought."

Now they looked stunned and I knew I must change the conversation as soon as possible. "What happened with Mr. Pattle after I'd gone, Bryony?"

"Er...nothing. I think he was quite relieved that Miss Morgan interrupted at that moment."

"But *we* weren't!" said Emily. "We were enjoying watching him writhe around like a squirmy little insect while Bryony pecked away at him like a big bird! In fact it was a shame that Miss Morgan had to come in!"

I didn't say anything but I so agreed with her.

Not surprisingly, Miss Morgan never came to find me again over the next few days and Mrs. Truman didn't say anything about what had happened. I stopped using the banister at the top of the stairs as a *barre* and I never went back into the room behind the laundry. The *other me* seemed to have gone, and it was a relief not to have to put up with the arguments in my head.

The only time that ballet ever came up was if we happened to be in the common room at the same time as Olivia and Maria, because as long as there was someone in there to admire them, they always talked about the show and demonstrated bits of their dance, pretending they were just practising. Apparently they'd persuaded a girl called Kate to take Olivia's part and Olivia was dancing Abi's part, because Abi's hamstring injury was still bad.

In the queue for lunch one time, Sasha and I were standing right beside the table where Maria was eating her lunch, and for once Olivia wasn't with her.

"Liv isn't half as good as you, Abi," she was saying to the girl opposite her.

So this was Abi. I hadn't seen her around school much, but now, simply eating her lunch, I thought how poised and graceful she looked. She ignored what Maria had just said, and I felt pleased, because I didn't like the way Maria was being so disloyal to someone who was supposed to be her friend. She and Olivia were as bad as each other.

Abi sighed and spoke heavily. "I don't get how my hamstring can be fine one minute but feel painful again the second I stretch my leg."

I felt so sorry for her at that moment, but then when Sasha and I saw her in the main library a day or two later, her face was altogether brighter. Sash and I were looking for a book we needed for English and Abi was having a whispered conversation with someone nearby. It was a minute or two before we realized that the girl she was talking to must be the one who was taking Olivia's place.

"I'm not making any promises, Kate," Abi was saying. "It just feels so much better this time that I'm certain I'll be able to manage the extensions in the dance."

"I can't tell you how happy that makes me," Kate replied. "I'm sure Olivia and Maria think I'm rubbish, and it would be great if you were back in the lead role. I told them dancing's just not my thing any more," she went on. "That's why I decided not to come back to ballet club this year."

"I'm coming to practise in the sports hall after school today to see what Miss Morgan thinks," Abi replied. "Ignore Olivia and Maria. You *are* good. I'm telling you!"

"Abi sounds really nice, doesn't she, Izzy?" said Sasha quietly when we were on our own again.

I nodded. "I feel sorry for Kate if Olivia and Maria are being unkind to her in rehearsals."

"Hey, why don't we go to the sports hall after school and ask if we can watch them rehearse?" said Sasha, her eyes shining like a little kid thinking of sneaking into her big sister's bedroom and taking something.

Surprisingly it felt safe to be talking like this with Sasha. I suppose it was because it was someone else's ballet world that we were so interested in, not mine.

"We'd better not actually go in," I quickly said. "But we could look through that little window round the corner from the main corridor."

So that's what we decided to do. And Sasha seemed to be just as into it all as I was when we were making our way to the sports hall after lessons had finished.

"I wonder why they're not rehearsing in the theatre," she said. "I'm sure Olivia said that's where the show is."

"I think the junior play is being rehearsed in there," I replied.

Sasha wrinkled her nose. "Well, why aren't the ballet group using the proper ballet studio, then?"

I explained that I was pretty sure the reason would be because they wanted a big room so they could imagine the stage better and work out their placings. And Sasha looked at me as though she was really impressed with my answer.

"You really know a lot about ballet, don't you, Iz?" she said quietly. And my mind flew back to the last time she'd said that, when the two of us had been sitting up in my bed, looking at photos at two in the morning. I didn't want that memory getting in the way of this new adventure Sasha and I were sharing, so I was glad we'd reached the side of the hall and I didn't have to reply.

A second later we were both peering through the little window that looked right into it. There was another larger window in the main corridor, but we'd chosen this little one because no one ever really came round the corner here, and also when you're actually in the hall you can't see if people are looking in at you from this one.

"Oh look, everyone's here. There's Abi talking to Kate," Sasha whispered. "And look, you were right about imagining the stage better – see, they've chalked out an oblong shape on the floor."

"It's quite a big area, isn't it?" I murmured, but I was more interested in watching what was going on.

I'd noticed Olivia and Maria warming up, and then there were four other girls standing around in leotards and tights, but no sign of Miss Morgan. We couldn't hear what any of the girls were saying, but when Abi put on the music it came over quite clearly. A moment later, the girls started doing individual stretches on the floor to the music to get warmed up, and it took me right back to my own classes. If Miss Amelia was here now, she'd be telling Kate to slow down. I could just hear her voice. *You'll sprain something working at that speed.* Abi, on the other hand, was stretching very slowly and thoroughly and avoiding putting any strain on her left leg. She looked almost professional, and it was thrilling to watch her.

Then we suddenly saw Miss Morgan go into the hall from the main corridor, her dance skirt flaring out as she ran with the lightest of footsteps across the hall. Immediately everyone stopped what they were doing and gathered around her. She must have been saying something important to Abi, because Abi kept on nodding hard, then shaking her head and looking serious. And as the others all got into their positions, with Olivia in the centre of the chalked rectangle, a proud look on her face that she was taking the main part, Abi sat on the floor ready to watch them.

I felt disappointed that I wouldn't be seeing her dance. Miss Morgan must have told her not to join in, in case she damaged her hamstring again. My heart raced as Miss Morgan changed the music and the dance began. It was almost as though I was actually taking part in the rehearsal myself, and I wished I could hear what Miss Morgan was saying every time she stopped the action and made a comment. At one point she demonstrated something to Olivia, and she looked so amazing that I was sure she must have been a professional dancer before she took up teaching. I could have watched her all day.

Every fibre of my body was absorbed in what was going on, so it gave me a shock when Sasha suddenly said, "I've just remembered, I said I'd go and help with the scenery painting again, Izzy. Do you want to come?"

"It's...okay, Sash. I'll just watch a bit more of this."

She smiled. "See you at supper then."

And then I was straight back into the rehearsal. The choreography was lovely, and Olivia was easily the best dancer there, then Maria. Kate and the others weren't turning out or extending their legs as much as they should, and they couldn't move as smoothly or expressively as Maria and Olivia.

After a while, Miss Morgan started pacing around with a big frown on her face as though she was deep in thought. I wondered if she was trying to decide whether to let Abi dance after all. And after a few seconds it looked as though I was right, because

Miss Morgan suddenly turned to Abi and said something, and in a flash Abi was reaching for her *pointe* shoes, then quickly putting them on and tying the ribbons. She looked so happy as she walked over to the chalked-out stage.

Kate seemed even more delighted. She gave Abi a big hug, then practically skipped off the stage area and stood to one side. Olivia looked furious as she moved out of the centre to the position that Kate had just had at the side, and Abi took up the central position.

This time, when the music started and Abi rose up onto *pointe* and raised her arms into fifth position, I felt such magic tingles all over me it was unbelievable. Even though she obviously wasn't dancing with her full energy, her performance was stunning. But she'd only been dancing for a few minutes when she stopped suddenly, clutching the top of her left leg at the back, and said something to Miss Morgan, before going to get herself a chair. Miss Morgan looked really concerned and so was I.

After that, the rehearsal just kind of fizzled out and I watched as everyone left the hall. Then I listened as they walked along the main corridor. Abi was saying, "I felt fine for ages, but now it's hurting like mad."

"You just need to make sure you give it enough rest," Miss Morgan replied. "I shouldn't have let you dance today. It's my fault."

As their voices disappeared into the distance, I knew I should be going too, but I couldn't quite tear myself away. In my head I was working out a different choreography with fewer extensions, so Abi's leg wouldn't be under such a strain. I needed to keep my eyes on the chalked-out stage and imagine all the girls dancing, or I couldn't do it properly. I stood there for ages, working out steps in my head and wishing I could write down all my ideas so I wouldn't forget them. After a while, as there was no one around, I went into Mrs. Truman's office and quickly grabbed a piece of paper and a pencil from her desk. Then I hurried back to my place around the corner and, once I'd had a final look at the imaginary stage, I started to write down what I'd worked out, as best I could.

The trouble was, I couldn't hear the music well enough in my head and I didn't dare go into the sports hall to play the CD, in case anyone came in and wondered what on earth I was doing. In the end, I waited till the whole block had been deserted for a good ten minutes. I knew I could be sure by then that no one would disturb me, because it was half past six and it wouldn't be worth anyone coming into the sports hall before supper.

So in I crept.

Chapter Seven

At first when I pressed play on the CD player and the music blared out, I went into a big panic and quickly turned it down, as it seemed far too loud for the hall. I guessed that was because I was all alone in such a vast room, so the background of silence was deeper than when there'd been loads of people in here.

I set the volume just loud enough to hear the music, then kicked off my shoes and took up my position on the pretend stage. I had to imagine I was *en pointe* like Abi, because I'd never done any *pointe* work, but it didn't matter. All that seemed to matter at that moment was feeling the dance that I'd just created for Abi coming alive. It was brilliant. There were no mirrors, no piano, no rosin box, no barres, no one judging me. I was back in my secret, private world, free to dance just for myself. I soon came to the end of the steps I'd worked out, and just carried on, making up more steps as I went along, dancing and dancing away without stopping.

And when the track finished, I put it on again, only this time I found myself dancing some of the steps of the original main part that I'd seen Olivia and Abi do. Then as the music came to a close, I did a big finish in the balance position that poor Abi hadn't been able to manage with her injured leg. My supporting leg felt strong and I held the position even after the last note had faded, because I was desperate to hold on to this moment for as long as possible. I don't know how long I would have stood there if the sound of clapping hadn't startled me and made me lose my balance.

Heart hammering, I turned to see Kate standing in the doorway. She came rushing over to me, crinkling with smiles. "I don't know your name, but whoever you are, that was *a-may-zing*!"

My mouth felt dry. It was lovely of her to give me such a compliment, but I was still totally embarrassed and upset at being discovered in the middle of my private world.

"Th...thank you."

"So what's your name?"

"Izzy."

"Izzy! Wow!" Kate laughed. "Sorry, I didn't mean, *Wow, Izzy, what a name!* I meant *wow* to the incredible dancing. Does Miss Morgan know about you? Does *anyone* know about you? I mean, why hasn't Miss Morgan ever mentioned you? She often talks about girls in the junior ballet club."

"I...I'm not in the ballet club."

"Not in the club! Why not? I'll tell Miss Morgan! In fact I'll tell her right now..."

"No!" I couldn't help blurting it out and I think I gave Kate a shock, because her eyes filled with alarm at the panic in my voice.

"No?" She looked at her watch and her expression softened. "No, you're right. She will have gone home. And actually we should be going to supper. I came back for the CD so I can practise in my boarding house. I'm not very supple..." Kate suddenly stopped mid-sentence and her eyes gleamed. She was staring at me as though she'd seen a ghost, but not a scary ghost – more a ghost she'd been dying to see. She spoke in a breathless whisper.

"I've had the most amazing idea…"

Something told me I wasn't going to like this idea one little bit.

"*You* could dance Abi's part!" The whisper turned to an excited flood of words. "You looked just as good dancing it in flats as Abi did *en pointe*, so that wouldn't be a problem. Olivia and Maria can stay in the roles they were originally given, because they look totally balanced like that and neither of them are anywhere near as good as Abi at her part anyway. That means I wouldn't have to be in the dance at all, so I won't let everyone down with my substandard dancing, and, hey presto, we have lift off! Woo!"

Kate's voice had risen to an excited whoop and then she grabbed both my hands and started dancing me round, sounding a bit like my friends but with a slightly different rhyme. "Izzy, whizzy, let's get dizzy!"

I couldn't help giggling. She was just so funny with her crazy happiness. But another part of me was scared stiff, and I let go of her hands and spoke in a gabble to make sure she really realized she *had* to forget her idea.

"Miss Morgan doesn't think I'm very good. I mean, she's right. I'm not. Abi's miles better than me. A million miles…obviously… She's a senior."

I broke off, because Kate was shaking her head slowly and staring at me as though I was melting away and she just couldn't grasp what was going on. "Miss Morgan doesn't think you're very good?" she asked, her face wrinkled up with bewilderment. She shook her head again and spoke slowly, emphasizing every word. "She cannot have seen you."

"She did. You see, I used to do ballet but I've given it up now."

Kate blinked, then gave herself a little shake before she fixed me with that same bewildered stare. But a moment later it disappeared. "Oh I get it! It's the thought of taking over a senior's part, isn't it? Listen, you mustn't worry about what the others think, honestly. Miss Morgan's the only one that matters." She glanced at the clock. "I've got to shoot back to my dorm before supper, but let's talk about it on the way." Now she was rushing over to the CD player and ejecting the CD, and then she was back with me, smiling and ushering me out of the door. "Look, all you have to do is turn up at the theatre after school tomorrow and you can show Miss Morgan and the others how you dance, exactly like you did just then. And I swear they'll be totally knocked out, and Miss Morgan can decide what's best!" She turned to me, eyes bright. "How's that for a plan?"

I suddenly realized Kate had stopped walking and was waiting for my answer because she was about to go off in another direction from the dining hall. I had to speak. I had to make her understand that there was no way I could just turn up at the theatre the next day. That I'd rather die than do that.

"I've...got gym club tomorrow."

"It doesn't matter if you miss clubs. Honestly. The teachers always say that if you've got something else going on, like a match or a rehearsal or something, you're allowed to miss clubs."

I swallowed. "But, you see, I don't really want to dance with the seniors when I'm not even in the *junior* ballet club..."

"Yes, but you should be. I don't get why Miss Morgan hasn't mentioned you to us lot when she's seen you dance." Kate looked at me carefully. "What did she actually say when she saw you?"

I looked down, trying to block out the awful memory. But I had to explain to Kate or she'd make me come to the theatre the next day and that would be unbearable. "She asked me if I wanted to have another go, but I didn't want to."

"What do you mean?"

"She…didn't think I was very good." My mind swung back to the Royal Ballet audition and I suddenly had to end this conversation. "I'd better go. Sorry…"

As I was walking away, Kate called after me, "Are you sure you won't just come along, Izzy?"

I turned round, but only for a second. "Yes, I'm sure. Sorry."

At lunchtime the next day, I saw Kate sitting down at a table just beside where Sasha and I were queuing. I didn't want her to notice me, because I was scared she might try to persuade me to go to the theatre again. Then Sasha would ask what we were talking about and she'd get to hear the whole story and she'd be sure to try and persuade me to do what Kate suggested.

I deliberately pointed out a picture to Sasha that was on the far wall of the hall, so we could turn right away from Kate.

"That's been there for ages, Izzy!" said Sasha, looking confused. "Have you only just noticed it?"

"No…but I've only just noticed how good it is."

We were shuffling along in the queue as we stared

at the picture, and any minute now we'd be past Kate, thank goodness. But then Sasha suddenly swung round the other way and pointed across the hall. "Look, that picture's even better. I love the colours, don't you?"

I had to look, and I could feel that Kate's eyes were on me.

"Hi, Izzy."

I swallowed and pretended I'd only just seen her. "Oh, hi!"

But then she was back into the conversation that was going on at her table and I relaxed. It was incredible. She hadn't said anything at all about dancing or ballet or rehearsals.

As I sat down at a table with the rest of my dorm and ate the delicious chicken chasseur, with my eyes on Kate across the room, a new wave of relief flooded over me. I'd never imagined she'd let the subject of me dancing go, just like that. But she must have had second thoughts and decided it was simply too late for me to join in the senior's dance now, when there was only a week and a bit left to go. Or maybe Abi's leg was better. Whatever it was, I was off the hook.

But I was still left with a mixed-up feeling inside my head. I suddenly realized I didn't mind the thought of watching the dance show any more.

I knew I'd feel emotional when it came to the ballet dance, but not in the kind of unbearable way I would have felt a few days ago. Something had changed. It wasn't so urgently important to keep my past completely shut out now. It was...weird.

All my friends were buzzing with chatter about how great the show was going to be, what with dressing up and being entertained all evening, and all the different sorts of dancing. Some Year Eights at the next table chimed in that whenever there's an event at Silver Spires for the whole school, it's always really exciting and buzzy, simply because of everyone being there. One girl said it was like suddenly having your whole family – with all your cousins and aunties and uncles and grandparents – for Christmas when you'd not seen them for ages. At first that thought gave me a little stab of sadness, as I remembered that Claire wouldn't be around over the Christmas holidays. But once I got over that, I actually started looking forward to the show.

"See that girl there," said Emily, breaking into my thoughts and pointing with her fork.

All five of us tried to follow the direction of her fork, but it was Bryony who pointed out that there were at least fifty possible girls that Emily might have meant.

"Come on, Ems, give us a clue!" she said, laughing.

"That one there!" said Emily. "She's talking to the girl next to her right now."

"Well that brings it down to about twenty possibles," said Bryony.

"Blonde hair...laughing...not laughing any more...putting her fork in her mouth..." said Emily, giving us a running commentary.

"You mean Natalie!" said Antonia.

"I don't know her name!" said Emily.

"What about her, anyway?" said Bryony, sounding exasperated.

"She's dancing a flamenco dance all on her own at the show. You know, with castanets and everything! I heard her telling someone."

I looked at Natalie and thought how brave and talented she must be. Or maybe she was simply full of confidence. I supposed that if you had bags of confidence, it wouldn't matter if you weren't absolutely brilliantly talented. But then as soon as I'd had that thought, I disagreed with myself. No, you had to have talent as well as confidence. If you were performing in front of an audience, you had to be the best. I remember Miss Amelia telling us that before every show I ever did. It was the thing that made me more nervous than anything. What if I wasn't the best? How could we *all* be the best?

As usual, I didn't like these memories, so it was a relief when Nicole turned to Emily.

"It's not like you to take such a big interest in someone dancing, Emily!"

Emily looked indignant. "I was only thinking how nice it'll be for Antonia to see someone doing an Italian dance."

We all burst out laughing and poor Emily sat there looking confused and even more indignant. "What's wrong with that?"

"The flamenco is a Spanish dance!" Bryony spluttered. "Get it right, Ems!"

I'd love to be like Emily. She's got the kind of pale skin that goes with her red hair and that goes pink easily, but she never seems to worry about it. She just laughed at herself. "Well, Spain's a bit nearer to Italy than England is, isn't it, so I expect you'll still enjoy it, Antonia."

And Antonia leaned over and awkwardly tried to give Emily a hug. "Yes, I weell love it!"

All through afternoon lessons, the six of us kept on remembering Emily's mistake and breaking out into giggles, which didn't go down very well with the teachers. And even when Sasha and I went to gym club we couldn't quite forget it.

It wasn't till gym club was over and we'd got changed and spent ages looking for Sasha's missing sock – which turned up in her skirt pocket for some unknown reason – that my lovely happy mood melted away. We were just going past the window in the main corridor when Sasha suddenly stopped and looked thoughtful. "Do you want to try out a few dance steps now there's no one here?" she asked in a gentle voice.

I didn't exactly freeze, but I felt a horrible fear. First Mrs. Truman had caught me dancing in the sports hall, then yesterday it was Kate. I couldn't risk it a third time. It would just be tempting fate.

"I can't. Mrs. Truman might come in," I quickly said.

"No she won't. There's no senior gym club this week."

"How do you know that? Are you sure?"

She nodded and smiled.

I looked through the window at the beautiful empty floor and remembered how much I'd loved dancing on that pretend stage the day before. Mrs. Truman had used some great music for our cool-down at the end of gym club and it might still be in the CD player. My legs were suddenly itching to dance.

"Okay," I said quietly, feeling that any louder might break the spell.

Sasha's eyes did their own little dance. "Come on, then."

A few moments later, I was moving to the music that we'd just used in gym club, only now it wasn't a cool-down exercise, it was ballet. I was trying out the steps I'd seen Abi and Olivia dancing the day before, then breaking into my own choreography that I'd worked out. They didn't quite match the music in the same way, but it still worked.

Sasha had turned the volume up high. She insisted that no one would be able to hear, since there was no one around anyway, and I was grateful to her because she'd made me relax for the first time in a long time, and it felt good to have Sasha closer to my secret private world. Not so lonely any more.

Then just when I was doing an *échappé sauté,* I felt that icy feeling and I knew without looking that Sasha wasn't the only one watching me. I could see that she was standing tensely and her eyes were big with alarm, so I stopped abruptly and my own eyes flew to the window. There was no one there and I wondered for a second if I was mistaken, but then

I remembered the little window, the one I'd used myself only the day before. Of course, I couldn't see properly, so I immediately turned to Sasha and noticed how pink her cheeks were.

"Is there someone watching me? Why do you look so embarrassed?"

She bit her lip, and her eyes did the smallest of darts towards the door. A second later the door opened and in came Kate with Miss Morgan. I stared at them, not knowing what to say or do.

"Sorry, Iz," said Sasha faintly, staring at the floor.

"You mean...you...knew they were watching?" I managed to stutter.

She didn't reply, because Miss Morgan was talking hurriedly. "Izzy, I don't think you did yourself justice the other day, you know. You're really very, very talented."

Suddenly I felt completely trapped, with nowhere to go. Even Sasha had been a traitor. My throat seemed to be closing and I knew I was going to cry. And then I did. I couldn't help it.

Kate came rushing across to me and put her arm round my shoulder. "Hey! What's all this? You're great. I just had to tell Miss Morgan to come to *you*, as you wouldn't come to *her*." She patted my arm, then let her hand drop, but she was trying to get me to look at her and I felt pathetic and babyish.

"Look, Izzy," Miss Morgan cut in. "I know you get very nervous about dancing in front of people, but you shouldn't, you know. You should be proud of yourself, with all this talent. You really are... exceptional."

Was I? Did she mean it? The words were starting to feel as though I ought to be believing them, but how could I? If it was true that I was *exceptional* then I would have got into The Royal Ballet School, wouldn't I? The path that led to my dream coming true.

Miss Morgan was looking at me gravely. "I really would like it if you'd agree to help out the senior ballet club, Izzy, because it looks as though Abi's strain is something more than that, and I've just seen how much of their dance you seem to have absorbed. It's incredible. I know you're good enough to join the group and the girls will be delighted. Really."

"Especially me!" said Kate. "Say you'll do it, Izzy. Please!"

I looked at Sasha. She was silent. No wonder. She must have still been feeling embarrassed. But that was nothing compared to what I was feeling, because something really awful had occurred to me. Maybe it wasn't just that Sasha knew I was being watched. Maybe it was worse than that, and she'd set me up deliberately. I just hoped and prayed that she hadn't. Best friends don't do that to each other.

But mixed in with all that hurt was my confusion. Miss Morgan and Kate were being so kind and complimentary, and Kate looked desperate for me to say yes. And suddenly I just didn't have the energy to fight any longer.

"Okay," I managed, in scarcely more than a whisper.

"Yessss!" said Kate.

And Miss Morgan took both my hands in hers and said, "Well done, Izzy. Come to the theatre tomorrow after school and we'll try out some ideas."

Chapter Eight

I went to bed that night feeling miserable because of what had happened when Sasha and I had left the sports hall. Almost as soon as we were out of the door, something had suddenly clicked in my mind about her sock turning up in her skirt pocket. It couldn't have got there on its own. No, it was definitely all part of a plan. Sasha needed to make sure we were last to leave the changing room. Why? Because she'd set me up. She'd given the game away when she'd said that Mrs. Truman wouldn't be coming back as there was no senior gym club. How did Sasha know that unless she'd spoken to a senior? And of course, I knew now exactly who that senior was. Kate.

It didn't matter that Kate thought I was good. It didn't even matter that Miss Morgan thought I was good. The Royal Ballet School didn't. All that mattered was that I'd never get my dream. And Sasha shouldn't have betrayed me. She shouldn't.

As I lay in bed, unable to sleep, I remembered how I'd rushed off down the corridor from the sports hall, calling sarcastically, "Thanks very much, Sasha. What a great friend you turned out to be!" and how Sasha had called after me in a voice that was nearly crying, "Yes, but, Izzy, I didn't..." Only I'd never turned back to find out what she was going to say. And then I'd deliberately sat on my own in supper, and as far away as possible from her during prep. And even though she'd tried to get me to listen to her twice more before bedtime, I'd told her I didn't feel like talking. So in the end, she'd had to give up. And that was when I realized how miserable I was. It was awful not being friends with Sasha, and it was also awful seeing the others watching us with big wondering eyes, as though they weren't sure whether to interfere or not.

I knew I'd been far too quick to get angry with Sasha, and lying in bed now, going through all that had happened, I knew really that she'd never want to hurt me. Whatever she'd planned with Kate, she probably thought it was for the best. So I made a resolution to say I was sorry first thing in the morning.

But when the morning came I couldn't do it, because something had changed overnight. Sasha must have given up on trying to apologize to me and wouldn't even look at me. It was awful. I never knew how much I relied on her friendship until I didn't have it.

So all through the morning I had a miserable time, latching on to Emily and Bryony because Sasha seemed to be going round with Nicole and Antonia. There was an awkward and embarrassing atmosphere whenever all six of us were together, because the other four were trying to pretend that everything was normal and yet it so *wasn't*.

By lunchtime I felt sick with nerves about going to the rehearsal that evening in a theatre I'd never even seen before and having to dance in front of a group of seniors including Olivia and Maria. Then after lunch, I went back to Forest Ash to drop off some books I didn't need for afternoon school and to collect a top that I thought would do for the ballet rehearsal, and also my tracky bums because I had absolutely no idea what I was supposed to wear as it hadn't even been mentioned. And it was when I was just about to key in the code to open the main front door to the boarding house, that out came Maria and Olivia.

"Oh, it's you. What's this we've been hearing about you coming to the rehearsal?" Maria said, giving me a cold look.

There didn't seem to be an answer to that question, so I just mumbled something about Miss Morgan asking me.

"Or was it Kate?" asked Olivia. "That girl's got some kind of complex that she isn't good enough to dance in the show. But she is. Experience counts for a lot in the world of ballet."

"Counts for everything," agreed Maria.

Olivia was still holding the Forest Ash door open for me, because if she let it go, it would shut and I'd have to key in the code to open it again. But she suddenly asked abruptly, "Are you coming in, or what?"

"Oh yes…" I hurried inside and realized that that was the end of the conversation. But just from the little they had said, it was obvious that Maria and Olivia didn't want me at the rehearsal, and basically thought I was far too young and inexperienced.

Their words kept on coming back to me throughout the afternoon, and by the time lessons finished I was a nervous wreck, wishing and wishing that Sasha and I were friends so I could ask her to come with me to the theatre. It would all seem so much easier with Sasha beside me.

Usually by the end of French, which is the last lesson, I'm desperate to get out of the classroom and stretch my legs and move my whole body after an afternoon of mainly sitting. But today I didn't have any urge to go tearing out of the classroom at all.

I glanced in Sasha's direction. Her face seemed paler than usual and her eyes looked big and anxious. Madame Poulain, our French teacher, was asking Nicole, who's a technical wizard as well as being so clever at everything else, if she'd mind helping her with a PowerPoint presentation that she was putting together. Madame Poulain wasn't sure how to set up the program, and wondered if Nicole might be able to help. Sasha and Antonia asked if they could stay behind too and Madame Poulain seemed really pleased to have so many volunteers. But I was sad, because I'd made another decision to apologize to Sasha, no matter what, as soon as French finished, and now I couldn't.

As I wandered off sadly, I turned back just once,

and our eyes met for a second before we both looked away. And I know it's stupid, but at that moment I felt as though Sasha could tell I was sorry for being horrible. I hoped so anyway.

The walk across to the theatre was awful. My legs felt so shaky, I doubted I'd be able to dance a single step, but I kept reminding myself that Miss Morgan thought I was exceptional. I also tried to hold in my mind a picture of Kate punching the air and saying "Yesss!" I think it was only these memories that stopped me from turning and running away.

It took all my courage to push the theatre door open, but the moment I stepped into the auditorium, there was Kate flying over to me with her lovely big friendly smile. She grabbed my wrist and pulled me across to the stage. "Here she is, everyone! Here's the little genius!"

I felt all squirmy inside when I heard those words and when I'd finished staring around at the incredible theatre, which was so grand and like something out of the West End, I realized that the rest of the seniors were eyeing me as though I was a disgusting wriggly specimen in the science lab that they had to study through their microscopes.

Miss Morgan didn't seem to be anywhere around and I so wished she'd quickly appear and give instructions and take control of everything. But she didn't, and instead it was Olivia who took charge.

"Well, I don't know what role Miss Morgan thinks Izzy's going to dance, because if Abi's leg is still bad, then obviously I'll be the one taking over her role and someone else will be doing mine."

No one else said a word, so Olivia carried on, raising her voice and gabbling a bit as though she had to get people to see things from her point of view. "And yeah, we all know Kate doesn't want to dance my part, but can you imagine how stupid it would look with Izzy dancing it? I mean, even if she knew all the steps and everything, and even if she could actually dance them properly, she's supposed to be a kind of mirror of Maria, and that wouldn't work, would it? They're completely different sizes."

Something had rushed into my body as Olivia had been talking, like a tornado that was whizzing round and round in the tightest knot just under my ribs in the place where Miss Amelia always told us to centre ourselves. I hated the way Olivia was addressing everyone as though I wasn't even there.

And then Maria took over, and the others all began nodding as she talked. "And if Abi's leg is better, which I reckon it will be, then there isn't any need for anyone extra anyway. It's pointless adding bits for no reason, because we don't have time to practise more steps, do we?"

"Never mind, Izzy," said another girl, giving me a nice smile. "It's great that we've got a junior coming through. Maybe you can dance your own little solo before our dance."

The knotted tornado stopped spinning for a short while, because at least someone had actually talked *to* me instead of talking *about* me. But with every word that was spoken, I'd felt more and more like a silly little kid thinking I could join in with the big girls, with no idea that I wasn't up to their standard.

"Hang on a sec, Leanne," said Kate. "Let's see what Miss Morgan says, shall we? I don't think you realize how good Izzy is."

"Yeah, I'm sure she's brilliant," said another girl, who I thought was called Rachel, "but—"

"She's only a junior," finished off someone else.

So now I knew that just about everyone, apart from Kate, thought it was an altogether ridiculous idea to have me joining in with their dance. And I wished a magic carpet could drop through the ceiling and the tornado inside me could whip me up and away from this theatre in a flash.

But instead of that happening, the door opened and in came Miss Morgan.

"Is Abi coming?" "How's Abi's leg?" "Is she going to be able to dance now?" came a general chorus.

I felt so spare standing there clutching my bag, and I kept my eyes on Miss Morgan, praying that she'd just quietly tell me that Abi was fully recovered so I wasn't needed after all and I could go. But she didn't. Instead, she put her hands up as though to show that she was about to make an important announcement. Then she came and stood right beside me.

"This is Izzy Carter, everyone." She turned and gave me a warm smile. "I'm sorry I wasn't here when you arrived, Izzy, but I had to speak to Miss Pritchard about rehearsal timings for the theatre." We all waited. "Now, girls, Kate and I watched Izzy dancing after her gym club yesterday and I have to say it was most impressive. You'll see what I mean in a moment. But first I want Izzy to watch *you* dancing. I shall take Abi's role myself for the moment, so we can keep the sense of symmetry we've got with Olivia and Maria mirroring each other, and Rachel, Leanne, Mimi and Debra balancing each other too."

Looks shot like lasers amongst the girls as they

took up their starting positions and Kate went across to put the music on.

"So isn't Abi coming?" Olivia asked in a sulky voice.

"She's seeing a sports injury specialist at the moment, but I'm sure she'll be along shortly. In the meantime..." Miss Morgan pointed to a seat in the front row of the auditorium. "Sit yourself down here, Izzy." Then she took up her own position in the middle of the stage and I drew my knees up and hugged them tight.

Watching Miss Morgan dance made me feel as though I was at Covent Garden. I've been there quite a few times to see The Royal Ballet Company dance, and I felt sure Miss Morgan was just as good as the dancers in that company, because she looked stunning on the stage and somehow made the others look better too. Olivia and Maria seemed lost in the dance, really extending their legs and holding their positions, and the four girls I didn't really know were perfectly in time with each other, which is so hard to do in ballet. There was no way the audience could think this dance was anything other than wonderful.

As they finished I broke into applause without thinking. Miss Morgan smiled at me and so did the girls at the back, but Olivia and Maria started talking to each other about some of the steps, as though I wasn't even there. Then a second later Olivia shot me a horrible look.

Miss Morgan was catching her breath, because Abi's part is really demanding and uses the whole stage. "Now," she said, "it's very daunting for someone as young as Izzy to come into this situation with all you seniors, and be expected to dance just like that, so let's start with a few steps all together like a class, so Izzy can warm up."

My whole body trembled at the thought of what was coming. "I don't have any ballet shoes or tights or anything," I said, praying that this might put a stop to all this, as then I wouldn't have to look at Olivia's and Maria's mean expressions any more.

"I thought that might be the case," said Miss Morgan. "But don't worry, I've brought spare leotards and tights, and I've got the right size shoes here." She handed everything to me. "Pop into the wings and get changed as quickly as you can."

I did as I was told, and all the while I could hear talking in fierce whispers going on in the auditorium, though I couldn't make out what was being said. And then the music started up again and I heard dancing feet, which I preferred to the sound of those cross voices, because I was totally sure they were talking about me. It was obvious no one except Kate wanted me here. I should never have agreed to come.

Creeping out of the wings, I reminded myself of a deer I'd once seen on a nature programme. It had been chased for miles until finally it was exhausted, but there was nowhere to hide. It was surrounded by lions and they were about to go in for the kill. I looked round at the girls, some practising onstage, two of them talking with Kate in the auditorium, and my body felt tired, with nothing more to give, like that poor deer.

"Right, Izzy," said Miss Morgan. "As we don't have *barres* in here, we'll do a few *pliés* in the centre. Prepare in first position, please, everyone."

In a flash, all the girls had found a space on the stage and I joined in, sinking into *demi pliés* and then full ones, following Miss Morgan's counts. It was so long since I'd worn a leotard and tights, and I loved the feeling of recovering something so familiar that had been missing. After clumsily trying to practise in my school uniform or my tracksuit, this felt wonderful. It was as though I was back in class with Miss Amelia, before I ever did the audition for The Royal Ballet. Before anyone ever told me I was a failure. I still felt as if I was surrounded by lions, but I wasn't quite so weak now.

After that we did a few *battement tendus* and *grands battements*, then Miss Morgan turned to me.

"Izzy, I know you know the first part of Abi's role, because I saw you dance it. Would you like to try it now?"

Someone tutted just loudly enough for me to hear. I was sure it was Olivia.

I gulped and walked to the centre of the stage, as Rachel and Leanne said, "Hang on a sec, we want to watch," and rushed down into the auditorium, followed by Mimi and Debra. So that just left Maria and Olivia, who had strolled to one side of the stage. Maria sat down cross-legged and Olivia folded her arms and tipped her head to one side. I only glanced at her for a second, but I could see her eyes were cold and unfriendly.

"What's she doing Abi's part for?" Olivia asked Miss Morgan in an accusing tone. "Are you saying that I'm not doing it now?"

"Look, Olivia," said Miss Morgan, with a sigh, "it might well be that the specialist says it won't harm Abi to continue using her leg even when it hurts a bit, in which case she can dance the role herself. But until we know that for sure, I don't want to waste a single second of this valuable rehearsal time, because if she's not able to dance then we need a plan B. Now you know as well as I do that Kate's heart isn't in it, so unless we completely change the choreography, which would take a lot of time and effort, then we need to juggle with what we've got. As you'll see in a minute, Izzy is an amazingly talented dancer, but obviously she's very small, so she can't just slot into the role dancing opposite Maria or we'd lose the symmetry."

Olivia sighed slowly and closed her eyes as if she couldn't believe what she was hearing. My head was spinning with thoughts and feelings. Poor Miss Morgan was just trying to make sure her ballet dance at the show was a success, and there wasn't time to change everything around. But Olivia must have hated the thought of giving up the lead role, especially to someone as young as me. This was the most awful position to be in. I'd finally accepted that Miss Morgan really did believe I was good, but now I had another test to pass. And it just seemed like one test too many. How ever was I going to dance a single step with such curious and hostile eyes on me? But I had to. Kate was about to press play. The music was going to start at any second. What if I messed up? It would be too awful to bear.

I turned out my right foot and stretched my left foot into a *dégagé*, then prepared my arms and took a deep breath to try to slow my heart down. And at that very moment the door opened and there stood Sasha. Our eyes met and she gave me a big smile and stuck both her thumbs up.

Immediately my whole body seemed to come to life and the energy soared up my legs to my shoulders and raced down my arms, as I held my head a little higher. I felt lighter and stronger, because I'd got my best friend back.

So I began, and I danced all the first sixty-four bars of Abi's role and then I couldn't remember what came next. But I only wavered for a second before I was back on track again, feeling in control. And the freedom of that feeling was the most wonderful thing ever. I could have danced and danced and danced, and all the while I kept a picture in my mind of Sasha's bright smile. It outshone Olivia's mean face easily. Nothing could touch me. Nothing, except for a small jarring sadness when the music came to the end and I finally had to stop dancing.

Then there was only my breath rushing into the silence. But a second later Kate was whooping and Miss Morgan and the girls in the auditorium were clapping loudly and Sasha had run right onto the stage to give me a hug. But over her shoulder I saw Maria and Olivia roll their eyes at each other and walk off into the auditorium, where they sat in the fourth row as though they didn't want anything to do with me.

"You were magic!" whispered Sasha into my ear, before she went across to join Kate.

Miss Morgan came over, put her hand on my shoulder and looked right into my eyes. "Lovely, Izzy. Well done!" Then she turned to the others and broke into a big smile. "I think maybe you see what I mean now, girls!"

A lot of chatter broke out then, and I didn't know where to look, so in the end I wandered off the stage with my head down.

But that was when Abi walked in, and everyone fell on her.

"What did the specialist say?"

"Is your leg okay now?"

"Can you dance?"

I knew what Abi was going to say before she spoke a word, because she looked so sad. "Apparently I'll really damage my hamstring if I do any of the extensions. So I've promised I won't dance until after the holidays, unless the choreography is completely changed so there aren't any extensions at all for my left leg." Then Abi noticed me. "Oh good! Kate said you'd agreed to come along." But she only managed the smallest of smiles.

"Bad luck, Abi," said Miss Morgan. She patted Abi's back and kept her hand there for a moment. "You'll be back to fighting fitness next term."

"I just feel as though I'm letting you down," said Abi.

"Don't be silly. It's not your fault."

Olivia got up out of her seat and went across to Abi. "It won't be half as good without you," she said in her forthright voice. Then she strolled back to Maria, flinging a horrible look in my direction as though to make quite sure that I knew what she meant about it not being half so good without Abi. But I understood all too well what she was trying to say. And it hurt.

Chapter Nine

After the rehearsal, Sasha and I talked and talked. I thanked her like mad for coming to the theatre and told her I was really sorry I'd been so horrible to her.

"I hated that you were so upset about what I did, Izzy," she said softly. "I just wanted to help. I knew something was wrong and I didn't know what, but I really wanted to make things right for you. It's so obvious that you love ballet, because whenever you talk about it, you kind of light up."

I was really grateful to Sasha and I felt as though this was the moment when I should be trying to explain to her about my past. But I couldn't do it. I would have had to say the "fail" word, and I wasn't ready for that. I didn't know if I'd ever be ready. So I just nodded and said, "Thank you."

Then when we walked back from supper that evening, Sasha said, "Everyone thought you were great at the rehearsal today, it was obvious!"

"Olivia and Maria didn't." I sighed. "They want either Olivia or Miss Morgan to do it."

"Just ignore Olivia and Maria." Then Sasha reminded me what had happened after Abi's announcement. Olivia and Maria had actually suggested the idea of Miss Morgan taking the lead role permanently, but Miss Morgan had insisted she definitely wasn't going to be in the dance and that rehearsals should continue with me. Then Abi had sat down to watch the rest of the rehearsal. "I was right next to Abi in the audience, Izzy, and she told me she really loved the way you danced the role. And so did I. You just got better and better. You'd learned the whole thing by the end of the session."

"But I still don't feel right about dancing with the seniors." I remembered that I'd be seeing Miss Morgan on my own after lunch the next day, because she'd asked me to go to a special extra practice.

"Maybe I should tell Miss Morgan that I feel out of place with the seniors, and see what she says."

"No," said Sasha firmly. "Just leave everything as it is. It'll be fine."

Poor Sasha. She was probably getting fed up with me and my silly anxieties. "Sorry, Sash. I won't mention it again."

She linked her arm through mine. "If only Maria and Olivia weren't so mean."

"I know."

After prep, the others went up to the dorm, but I went along to the internet room to e-mail Mum. I suddenly felt like pouring out the whole story to someone who was close to me but wasn't at this school. I felt sure it would help me to sort out my anxieties and hopefully make me feel better.

But when I went to write the e-mail, I found there was one from Max.

Hi Iz,

Hope you're okay. Still missing Claire. Pathetic, isn't it? Thinking I might give her a ring. Not sure though. Holly sends love. So do M and D.

Max xx

I couldn't help feeling another little burst of

happiness at the way Max kept asking my opinion. Well, he hadn't exactly *asked* for it, but he was telling me what he was thinking of doing, and that was amazing, considering how he always used to keep me in my place. It was like I'd suddenly grown up in his eyes. I thought back to the conversation I'd had with my friends and remembered how Emily had immediately said he ought to phone Claire, as though it was the most obvious thing in the world. Good old Emily, thinking of it straight away, when Max was only just coming round to the idea all this time later. I knew I ought to encourage him, so I quickly wrote back, saying I thought it was a great idea because if he was missing her then he must still want to go out with her.

It was when I was about halfway through that the door to the internet room opened and in came Olivia. Immediately I felt myself knotting up inside again. Just the sight of her made me all stiff and shaky.

"Hi," she said, dropping casually into the seat next to mine and switching on a computer. "So have you...decided what to do?"

She was watching her screen spring into life and she sounded quite bored already. I wasn't sure what she meant.

"De...decided?"

"Yeah. Have you decided whether to go for the solo or to stick with the seniors?"

I hadn't even realized I was supposed to be deciding, but now that she mentioned it, perhaps I was. It was true that Miss Morgan had never actually said, *Right, Izzy, you're taking over Abi's role in the senior ballet club's dance. And that's that.*

"Er...I'm not sure."

"Yeah, it's difficult for you, coming along to a senior club when you're only Year Seven."

I didn't reply, but I could feel myself getting hot. I went back to my inbox and started to read a nice chatty message from my aunty, as there was no way I could concentrate on finishing my e-mail to Max now.

Out of the corner of my eye I could see that Olivia was typing, and when she spoke next it was still in that same casual tone. "It's not your fault though."

I stopped reading abruptly. "Wh...what's not my fault?"

Olivia was shaking her head and looking gravely at the computer and at first I thought it was because of something she'd seen on the screen, but then she carried on about me. "You can't help being so young.

It's not your fault that you've not been dancing as long as the seniors. And that you're..."

I swallowed and felt my throat hurting. "And that I'm what?"

She suddenly stopped what she was doing and whipped round to look at me properly. I felt like a little kid interrupting the grown-up who was doing something important. "Well, the others were on about how funny it would look with one dancer so much smaller than all the others, that's all."

I closed down the e-mail and got up shakily. "I'd better go..."

"Oh...right. See ya then."

I didn't say anything to Sasha about that terrible conversation. She would just repeat that I ought to ignore Olivia. But how could I?

That night I lay in bed and tried to put myself in Olivia's shoes. It was impossible, so I tried to imagine I was one of the others – say, Rachel. How would I feel if a little Year Seven came along and joined in with my senior ballet club dance and then took over the main part?

It was no good – I couldn't even put myself into Rachel's head. All I could think about was how magic it had been to let my body do what it wanted to do and dance out in the open, feeling the music lifting me.

But that was selfish and I had to think about the others. Olivia had really spelled it out to me. I didn't fit in with the seniors. I knew now what I had to do. The very next day I would go and tell Miss Morgan that I didn't want to join in with their dance.

The following day I didn't tell Sasha about my decision to talk to Miss Morgan. At lunch, I just asked her to save me a place in music that afternoon in case I was late, then off I went to the theatre. My footsteps were slow and I felt weak with nervousness at the thought of what I was about to say. I took a deep breath as I opened the door.

"Izzy! Excellent timing! I've only just got here myself. And I've worked out—"

"Miss Morgan?" I knew I was being rude interrupting her, but if I didn't say what I had to say immediately, I'd never be able to say it.

"Yes?" She looked startled.

"I've decided I don't want to do Abi's role. I think I'm too young and not really good enough..."

"Of course you're good enough! What's made

you have second thoughts, Izzy? You seemed so positive yesterday."

I'd practised my words and I made sure I spoke firmly so she really knew I meant it. "I agree with the others that it would be better if a senior did it."

Miss Morgan frowned. "It doesn't have to be just the senior club or just the junior club or just *any* club in a routine. There are people doing other sorts of dance in the show who don't belong to a club at all."

"But I think Leanne was right and it would be better if I did something separately…"

Miss Morgan sighed. "Come and sit down, Izzy."

I did as I was told and waited while she stared straight ahead for a few seconds. Then she began to speak. "I want to tell you what I saw when you first danced for me in the ballet studio, Izzy."

I bit my lip.

"I saw a girl with the most extraordinary talent and the most awful lack of self-confidence, and I thought to myself, I wonder what's happened to make this girl so full of self-doubt. You looked like a rabbit in the headlights, Izzy, and I hated to see you upset like that, so I let you go. And then I went straight to the headmistress."

A gasp came out of me. Ms. Carmichael, the Head of Silver Spires, was the only person who knew that I came here because I didn't get into The Royal Ballet School. I hoped like mad that she'd forgotten. Surely she wouldn't remember every single detail about every single girl who came to her school.

"Ms. Carmichael looked in the files that she holds about all the students and told me that you'd decided to come to Silver Spires in preference to The Royal Ballet School. That's all she said, but it was all I needed to know. It explained everything, you see."

Suddenly I had to put Miss Morgan right. "It wasn't that I decided to come here instead of The Royal Ballet. I did the audition for The Royal Ballet because it was my dream to go there. But I failed, and...so that's why I came here."

At last I'd said it. I hung my head with shame. Now Miss Morgan would realize that I wasn't good enough to be a professional or to dance with the seniors.

There was a silence that seemed to go on for ages, and then she sighed. "Do you know who you remind me of, Izzy?"

I shook my head and kept my eyes on the ground.

"Me. You remind me of myself. I auditioned for

The Royal Ballet when I was your age and I didn't get in either. I was heartbroken for a while, but I kept up my studies at another ballet school and eventually I became a ballet teacher..."

"You mean you never became a professional dancer?" I was looking straight at her now, because I was so shocked by what she'd said.

"No, but I've danced in lots of shows on lots of stages, and I've also got a degree in dance studies as well as my teacher's qualification, and I'm very happy now that I didn't get into The Royal Ballet."

Being good enough to dance with The Royal Ballet had been my ambition for so long that I couldn't believe what Miss Morgan was telling me. "Why?" I blurted out.

"Because the life of a professional dancer is so tough and so very, very restrictive. I've got a partner, I've got two lovely children, we have fun at weekends – sometimes we all go riding, and I don't have to worry about getting injured – and I don't have to make sure I definitely do a class every day. I've truly got the best of both worlds. I love to go to ballets and to choreograph dances. And most of all I love the fact that my ballet doesn't have to be all or nothing. Ballet is just one part of my life. Not all of it."

I'd been staring so hard at Miss Morgan that my eyes were starting to fill with tears. Or maybe it wasn't because of staring. Maybe the tears were just ready to come anyway. I had to be sure that I really understood what she was saying.

"So you're... actually glad you didn't get into The Royal Ballet?"

She nodded.

"Didn't you feel like a failure at first?"

"Yes, I did. And then my teacher told me that every year there are only twelve places for girls in Year Seven at The Royal Ballet School and just to be considered good enough to audition meant I was in the top hundred best ballet dancers in the country, so I ought to be happy, and I definitely *wasn't* a failure."

As Miss Morgan spoke, I felt as though a heavy weight was dropping off my shoulders. I couldn't speak though, because the tears were rolling down my face and I realized I was actually crying. I think it was the relief that suddenly I didn't have to worry about being a failure any more. I didn't have to put ballet behind me. I could be like Miss Morgan and have it strongly in my life without it being my absolute whole life.

Miss Morgan smiled at me and held my hand

firmly. "Just suppose, Izzy Carter, that The Royal Ballet School phoned your mum right now and said that someone had dropped out, so there was a place for you, because you were number thirteen and only just missed passing the audition by one place. You could pack your bags right now and go to London to The Royal Ballet School. What would you say?"

I felt a terrible sadness filling up my whole body and every corner of my mind. I couldn't leave Silver Spires. Not now. I loved it. I couldn't leave all my friends and lovely Emerald dorm. And most of all, I could never leave Sasha. Never.

Miss Morgan was waiting for me to reply. I wasn't crying any more, so it was easy to speak. "I'd say, *No thank you. I prefer it here.*"

"Well there you are then." Miss Morgan squeezed my hand tight, then let it go as she pulled a face at me, pretending to be cross. "Now will you stop thinking you're a failure and start enjoying ballet again. Dance whenever you can. Join the junior ballet club, let everyone know that ballet is your passion, and most important of all, let's get on with practising your part for the show!" I did a gulpy breath, the kind you do when you've been crying, and Miss Morgan carried on talking, but more seriously again. "You know, Izzy, Abi said that the one good thing about injuring her hamstring was that it gave us the chance to find *you*. She thinks you are amazingly talented, Izzy, *and* she wants to work out a special duet for the two of you for next term. She's full of plans, you know."

"So she doesn't mind me taking her place?"

"No, absolutely not. Abi's a lovely generous soul who just wants everything to be right. It's true that there are one or two students who will always be jealous of other people's success, but that's not *your* problem, Izzy, so just ignore it."

"That's what my friend Sasha said."

Miss Morgan nodded as she got up. "She's a very wise friend, in that case. And now, let's get to work!"

So we did. And I loved every single minute of it.

After school that day, none of us had clubs and we were all just hanging out in the dorm doing nothing in particular. I felt happy, because the others were so relaxed now that Sasha and I were friends again. Not one of them had said a single word about us falling out and no one asked us any questions, they just seemed to accept that whatever was wrong had been put right, and I felt so grateful to all of them for that.

Antonia and Nicole were sitting cross-legged on the carpet, knitting. Antonia said that her grandmother had taught her how to knit at half-term and she was knitting a tank top in a beautiful dark green. But she'd also brought back knitting needles and wool for Nicole to make one exactly the same, only in dark blue. It had been Nicole's birthday at half-term, and we all thought what a fabulous present it was.

I watched the two of them with their heads so close together studying the knitting pattern, and got a sudden memory of how they'd really not liked each other at all at the beginning of term. It was all a huge misunderstanding, but it was really awkward at times for the rest of us until they sorted everything out between the two of them. Then shortly afterwards, Antonia said she wanted us all to have a "truth talk". Her English wasn't half so good then as it is now, but we all knew exactly what she meant. She just wanted to confide in us, and the name "truth talk" stuck because it was so sweet.

Bryony and Emily were on Emily's laptop looking at pictures that she'd downloaded of her pony back home in Ireland. Their heads were close together too, and I thought how amazingly different their hair was – Emily's in thick unruly auburn waves and Bryony's short and dark and shiny.

And when my eyes went round to Sasha, who was reading on her bed, I suddenly felt as though these friends of mine should know what Miss Morgan now knew. Especially Sasha.

"Can we have a truth talk?" I asked quietly.

"Of course!" said Antonia, jumping up. Nicole got up straight after her and they both climbed up to my bed.

"Come on!" said Antonia to the others. "Thees ees the bed to belong to!"

It was unusual for Antonia to come out with funny English these days, but no one corrected her or said anything about it, and I guessed they were too busy wondering what it was I wanted to say. We all managed to squash on the bed somehow, then everyone was quiet and five pairs of eyes were all on me.

"I know I've been a bit weird about...ballet and everything..."

No one spoke. They all just waited.

"Well, anyway, I think I'm okay now, because I've talked to Miss Morgan and she's kind of in the same boat as me."

Sasha's eyes widened.

"She was telling me that when she was my age she auditioned to go to The Royal Ballet School and she didn't get in, and she felt a failure too…"

I bit my lip and looked at Sasha, because I felt as though I needed someone to speak then. But it was Emily who actually spoke first.

"You mean you nearly went to The Royal Ballet School? My second cousin tried to get in and failed, and he's a *boy*! He told me it's fifty times more difficult for a girl, and your teacher will only ever think of putting you in for that school if you're mega-brilliant at ballet, you know – like the best in the country!"

"Oh wow, Izzy! You must be amazing!" said Bryony.

"Well I already knew you were brilliant, just from watching you move," said Nicole.

"And I also," said Antonia.

"Thank goodness you didn't get in," said Sasha quietly, "or I'd be sitting here with a completely different best friend who might not be as nice as you and then I'd be totally miserable."

There was a pause before we all cracked up laughing, and I gave Sasha a big smile because that was such a nice thing to say.

"I think we ought to put some of your ballet pics up now," she whispered to me when the others had got off my bed and there were just the two of us left.

So we went through them all together and Sasha started to arrange them on the pinboard, working from the outside in until there was space for just one more, right in the middle. "Look, this little place is perfect for that photo of you in your last show, Whizz."

But for some reason I didn't want that photo up for all to see. I wrinkled my nose. "Isn't there anything else?"

"Oh, why not that one of you? It's great!"

How could I explain? "Because…I feel as though I've been two people until today – the *new me* and the other me. And that photo reminds me too much of the *other me*. And I don't want to be reminded of that, now there's only *one* me."

Sasha laughed. "Whatever you say, Iz!"

And I knew I hadn't explained it very well, but it was true. There *was* only one me.

The real me.

Chapter Ten

It's nine fifteen in the evening and I'm standing in one of the wings of the theatre, with Miss Morgan, Rachel, Leanne, Mimi and Debra. In the wing opposite are Olivia and Maria. We're all wearing different-coloured leotards and flesh-coloured tights, and we've got our hair scraped back tightly. My own leotard is silver and I absolutely love it.

We're keeping our limbs moving very gently after the warm-up we've already done. On the other side of the heavy dark red curtain is just about every girl in the whole school, and lots of teachers too. They're all chattering in loud, excited voices about the dance act that's just finished, the one before us. It was Natalie dancing the flamenco, and even from the wings I thought she looked brilliant.

I'd watched the first half of the show with my friends in the auditorium. There was loads of jazz and tap and disco and Latin American, and it was all wonderful. The louder the music and the more energetic the dancing, the more the audience seemed to love it. So right now, knowing that any minute we'd be dancing our slow, smooth ballet dance, it was very, very scary.

"What if they don't like it?" Mimi asked Miss Morgan, her teeth chattering with fear. "It hasn't got a beat. It's not as cool as the other stuff."

"Don't be silly. You'll be brilliant and they'll love it," said Miss Morgan firmly.

"But it's so different from everything else in the programme," said Debra. "And I definitely heard someone in the audience groaning a moment ago when they saw what was next. They said, 'Oh no, not *ballet*!'"

I was already nervous, but at those words of Debra's, I started to feel sick.

"Okay, girls, get into your positions," said Miss Morgan. "And have faith in yourselves. If the audience don't love you, I'll eat my hat!"

"I hope you've got an edible hat," said Rachel shakily as she moved onto the stage. I followed her, and took up my position in the centre at the front, noticing that, as usual, Maria and Olivia weren't looking at me at all.

We'd only had two rehearsals all together after my practice on my own with Miss Morgan, because we didn't need any more than that. The dance was ready for the show. But neither Maria nor Olivia had ever said a single word to me from start to finish during those rehearsals. Abi had watched both times and given me loads of compliments at the end, and the other four seniors always patted me on the back and said, "Well done." But Olivia and Maria made it all too clear they didn't like me being in the show. And I had to work hard on clearing my mind of them as I prepared my starting position with my head bowed.

We stood like seven statues on the dark stage as our music began and the noise on the other side of the curtain slowly quietened. Then as the curtains opened, there was complete silence. A second later the stage was flooded with bright light and I was glad I couldn't see the faces in the auditorium. I started to imagine there was nobody there and that I was dancing for myself. I knew the others would be gliding in intricate patterns behind me, which looked so beautiful, while I simply had to raise my head very slowly, and then my arms, and then one leg out to the side until my toe was pointing up higher than my head. It was probably the hardest step in my whole part, because I had to hold my balance for so long, but I did it, and I heard gasps from all over the audience, which I hadn't been expecting. So when the music swelled and it came to my leaps and spins, I felt as though I was being lifted right up. And somehow there was an energy amongst the seven of us dancing our hearts out that had never been there when we'd rehearsed. Maybe the music was louder, or maybe it was the bright lights, or just our nervousness, but we were different from how we'd been in rehearsal, and I didn't want the dance to end because the audience were different too. They seemed stunned, and even when the last note faded and we stood in our final positions, there was a breathtaking silence before the applause rang round the theatre in massive, vibrating waves. No one in the audience spoke, they all just clapped and clapped. And then they were on their feet, still clapping.

I reached out to the sides as Miss Morgan had instructed me to do, so that Maria and Olivia would hold my hand on either side and the other four join on the two ends of the line for the final bow. We'd only practised this once and Maria and Olivia had let my hands drop instantly at that practice, as though they couldn't bear holding hands with a Year Seven. But this time they kept holding tight. Then we all had to take four steps backwards at exactly the same moment, raise our joined hands and drop into another bow, before the curtains closed. And that's exactly what happened.

Miss Morgan rushed onstage a moment later and hugged us all. She said she was so proud that she could burst into tears. We all started to leave the stage, but then we realized the clapping was still as loud as ever, even after all this time, so Miss Morgan told us to get back into our line, and the curtains started to open once more.

"*You* come in the line too, Miss Morgan," said Maria, letting go of my hand, to encourage Miss Morgan to join us. And that's how we were when the audience saw us. A massive cheer went up as Miss Morgan took a bow with us. But she only stayed for a moment, and even after she'd hurried back to the wings the audience was still cheering and clapping. And next thing I knew, Maria had let go of my hand again and when I glanced sideways, I saw that she was giving me a genuine smile. "Take a bow on your own," she whispered.

She got the others to move back so I was left alone at the front of the stage. As I did a deep curtsy, so many whoops came out of the audience, and flashes from people's cameras and phones, that I felt like a real star. But I couldn't stay on my own – it wasn't fair on the others. So I went back to hold their hands and bring them all forwards for one last bow, before the curtains finally closed.

"I should think that Royal Ballet School must be kicking themselves!" said Emily as we made our way up to Emerald dorm later that evening, going very slowly because we were all texting out parents about the show. I'd already texted Mum, and she'd replied with just three little words, except that one of them took up about three lines of the screen.

I'm soooooooo
ooooooooooo
ooooooooooo
proud!

It was really lovely and flattering the way my friends had talked and talked about our ballet piece ever since the end of the show, saying it was the best part of the whole show and that everyone had thought so.

"You just shocked us all!" said Nicole.

"Knocked us out!" added Bryony.

"Knocked us out?" asked Antonia, in big alarm.

"It's just a saying," explained Sasha, laughing.

Then we all got ready for bed, and just before we had to hand in our phones for the night, mine bleeped that I'd got two texts.

"Oh, it's from my brother!" I said, scanning the first message.

Just wanted u 2 know Claire nd I r back
together.
I missed her 2 much. All a stupid mistake!
Mum says ballet was big success. Congrats!
Max x

My eyes filled with tears of happiness. I understood more than anyone just how wrong it felt when you missed something with all your heart. It wasn't easy reading the second text through my tears.

Got ure no. from Sasha. U were total star.
I never thought ud b able 2 do it.
I was wrong. Luv Olivia xx

* * *

I knew I wouldn't get to sleep for ages that night because I was far, far too happy for sleep. But it didn't matter, because the next day was Sunday and we were allowed a lie-in. And then there was only one more week of term before the Christmas holidays. Sasha and I had made big plans to see each other, even though our families lived nearly two hundred miles apart. I was so happy that our parents had agreed to that, because I knew I'd miss her terribly otherwise.

We all lay in bed talking and talking, then just when my eyes were beginning to droop a bit, I turned my head to look at my pinboard as I did every night, and immediately sat up in big surprise because something had changed. Right in the middle, the blank space had been filled with a picture of me wearing a silver leotard and smiling as though I owned the world.

"What...? When...? How...?" I began in big confusion.

"Sasha took it," laughed Emily. "Then Bryony rushed off at the end – as she's the fastest runner," she added, "and transferred it to a computer and printed it out! So, hey presto, we have the one and only...Izzy!" Emily had spoken in an over-the-top dramatic voice and was pretending to raise her glass, as though she was at a grand party, proposing a toast.

The others laughed and joined in the fun, raising their own imaginary glasses. "To the one and only Izzy!" they chorused.

And Sasha and I exchanged our own special smile, because we both knew just how true those words really were. Ballet had found its place in my life again, and at long last I really had finally found *the one and only me.*

Want to know more about the
Silver Spires girls?

Or try a quiz to discover which
School Friend you're most like?

You can even send Silver Spires e-cards
to your best friends and post your own
book reviews online!

It's all at

www.silverspiresschool.co.uk

 Check it out now!

Izzy's Dance Fact File

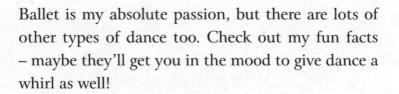

Ballet is my absolute passion, but there are lots of other types of dance too. Check out my fun facts – maybe they'll get you in the mood to give dance a whirl as well!

★ All sorts of dance styles are practised and performed in the UK, including African, ballroom, belly dancing, body-popping, break-dancing, classical ballet, contemporary, flamenco, historical, Irish, jazz, jive, line dancing, national and folk, salsa, square-dancing, street dance, tango and tap. Phew!

★ Most ballerinas wear out 2-3 pairs of pointe shoes in a week – for some performers, a single pair is not enough to get through a whole performance!

★ In Bharatanatyam, Kathak and Odissi – different forms of classical Indian dance – dancers wear heavy anklets of multiple bells called *gungru* or *ghungroo* to emphasize the rhythms of their feet. Dancers can wear up to two hundred bells – a hundred on each ankle.

★ A single ballet tutu for a performance can cost over £1000 and take 75 hours to make.

★ Girls who take part in Irish dancing competitions nearly always wear very curly wigs. Wigs were originally introduced for seriously competitive dancers who would go to a *feis* (Irish dance competition or festival) every week and found that constantly curling their hair damaged it. But the wigs caught on like wildfire – even though they're quite uncomfortable to wear!

★ Dance marathons were very popular in America in the 1930s. Marathoners danced for hours and sometimes days at a time to compete for cash prizes. Americans Mike Ritof and Edith Boudreaux hold the world record. From 29th August 1930 to 1st April 1931, they danced for 5,148 hours and 28 minutes – that's 214 days!

★ Dancing is such great fun and it gets you fit too! Instead of going to the cinema, try going dancing with your friends or making up a routine to your favourite song – an hour's dancing can be the equivalent of going for a 6km walk. If you do high-energy salsa dancing, you'll get an even better workout!

Izzy

Now read on for a sneak preview of

Dreams at Silver Spires

"**O**uch!"

What's Bryony doing attacking me like this? She's supposed to be my best friend. I stopped staring at the cloudy grey sky through the gap between the treetops, and raised my eyebrows at her in a vague kind of way.

"Ems, come back from whatever planet you're on!" said Nicole, laughing. "We've been trying to attract your attention for ages!"

And when I looked round I saw that it wasn't only Bryony and Nicole who were finding me amusing, but all of my little group of friends.

"What were you daydreaming about, anyway?" asked Sasha.

It was true I'd been miles away, thinking about my other best friend, my beautiful horse, Barney, who lives back home in Ireland. I was imagining myself galloping him across open fields on a beautiful summer evening when all the work on our farm had been done – well, all the work *I* had to do at least, because Mum and Dad and my big brother Will always work till really late in the summer.

But how could I explain all that to my friends? None of them have got much of a clue about horses, and they certainly don't know the first thing about farming. I still love them dearly, though, because the six of us have been together in the same dormitory here at Silver Spires Boarding School for Girls for a term and a bit now, and the others don't seem to mind that I'm always either daydreaming or, if you press my other button, rushing to get out in the fresh air. They're not bothered that I don't care about fashion or that I'm not the best in the world as far as lessons are concerned. They all just accept the way I am. Well, apart from a few times like right now, when I think I *do* get on their nerves.

But I always know how to bring them round. "I was daydreaming about winning the lottery and just wondering which friends I might take with me on my trip to see the wonders of the world!"

That had exactly the effect I expected. Izzy and Sasha stopped trying to keep warm by jogging on the spot and gave me big beaming smiles, while Antonia and Nicole both shuffled close to me and linked their arms through mine, and Bryony started batting her eyelashes about two centimetres away from my face in a totally over-the-top way, which looked so funny, knowing what a tomboy she is. We must have seemed like a really weird little group standing in the middle of the main lane that runs through the Silver Spires grounds.

"Okay, I'll take you all!" I said, sighing a bit and pretending they were a lot of pestering children that I had to keep quiet somehow.

When they'd finished being amused by me for the second time in two minutes, Izzy started doing vigorous star jumps. "How come you don't feel the cold, Emily?"

"I'm just used to it, I suppose," I told her with a shrug. Then I looked at my watch. "Surely a few of the guests should have arrived by now, shouldn't they?"

Well that sent Izzy and Sasha straight back into their big excitement zone. "I can't wait to see them. I've got so many questions!" said Sasha.

"Me too!" squeaked Izzy. "And I bet they've got loads to ask each other, too. I mean, it'll seem so strange meeting up for a grand reunion party after all these years."

And then Nicole and Antonia were joining in with the buzz, while Bryony and I stood quietly to one side. Neither of us was looking forward to the afternoon in quite the same way as our friends were, and we'd only really come outside to look out for the guests arriving because the others had wanted us to.

"I suppose it'll be quite interesting when we get talking to people, but I'm not as excited as the others, are you?" I asked Bryony quietly.

She's a very thoughtful person, my best friend, so she didn't answer me straight away. But then her face suddenly brightened. "I'm looking forward to the tea!"

"Me too!" I said, giggling. "All those totally fab home-made cakes and biscuits!"

"I hope they decorate the hall to make it very grand," said Antonia, joining in with us now. "And use Silver Spires's best silver teapots and china!" she added, with a dreamy look in her eyes.

"Is that what your dad would do in his restaurant in Italy?" I asked her, because I'm interested in how the different countries all have their own traditions and ways of doing things.

"Afternoon tea isn't a custom in Italy, like it is in England," Antonia replied. "But yes, it's true, Papà makes his restaurant look extra-specially wonderful for important occasions."

Just about every time Antonia speaks I think how much her English has improved. When she joined Silver Spires with all the rest of us Year Sevens last September, she had trouble with lots of English words and she had a really strong Italian accent. But now you only notice her accent a bit. Nicole, her best friend, has helped her loads with the language. Antonia's also taught Nicole quite a bit of Italian, which Nicole has picked up really quickly, as she's the brainiest one in our group.

When Antonia started talking about decorations, I'd been imagining the big hall here in the beautiful old main building of Silver Spires full of women in their sixties all enjoying their grand reunion, introducing themselves to each other and chatting away about what they'd done since they'd left Silver Spires all those years ago. Now I suddenly felt myself wanting to break into giggles again.

"Isn't it funny the way everyone always calls them old girls?" I spluttered. "I mean it sounds kind of rude, doesn't it, to say, 'A load of old girls are coming to a reunion party at Silver Spires'!"

"Well, if you put it like that it sounds rude. But that's exactly what they are, aren't they?" said Nicole. "Old girls. It's really amazing that they're all coming back to meet up after fifty years."

"Yes, they might not even recognize each other," said Sasha. "It'll be so weird for them all, won't it? They'll be comparing notes about what boarding houses they were in and what their housemistresses were like…"

"Just think," I said, as something suddenly dawned on me, "this party could be *us* in fifty years' time."

To find out what happens next, read

Dreams at Silver Spires

Complete your
School Friends
collection!

First Term at Silver Spires   ISBN 9780746072240

Katy's nervous about going to boarding school for the first time – especially with the big secret she has to hide.

Drama at Silver Spires   ISBN 9780746072257

Georgie's desperate to get her favourite part in the school play, but she's up against some stiff competition.

Rivalry at Silver Spires   ISBN 9780746072264

Grace is eager to win in the swimming gala for Hazeldean – until someone starts sending mean messages about her.

Princess at Silver Spires   ISBN 9780746089576

Naomi hates being the centre of attention, but when she's asked to model for a charity fashion show, she can't say no.

Secrets at Silver Spires   ISBN 9780746089583

Jess is struggling with her schoolwork and has to have special classes, but she can't bear to tell her friends the truth.

Star of Silver Spires   ISBN 9780746089590

Mia longs to enter a song she's written in the Silver Spires Star contest, but she's far too scared to perform onstage.

❀ About the Author ❀
Ann Bryant's School Days

Who was your favourite teacher?

At primary it was Mr. Perks – we called him Perksy. I was in his class in Year Six, and most days he let me work on a play I was writing! At secondary, my fave teacher was Mrs. Rowe, simply because I loved her subject (French) and she was so young and pretty and slim and chic and it was great seeing what new clothes she'd be wearing.

What were your best and worst lessons?

My brain doesn't process history, geography or science and I hated cookery, so those were my least favourite subjects. But I was good at English, music, French and PE, so I loved those. I also enjoyed art, although I was completely rubbish at it!

What was your school uniform like?

We had to wear a white shirt with a navy blue tie and sweater, and a navy skirt, but there was actually a wide variety of styles allowed – I was a very small person and liked pencil-thin skirts. We all rolled them over and over at the waist!

Did you take part in after-school activities?
Well I loved just hanging out with my friends, but most of all I loved ballet and went to extra classes in Manchester after school.

Did you have any pets while you were at school?
My parents weren't animal lovers so we were only allowed a goldfish! But since I had my two daughters, we've had loads – two cats, two guinea pigs, two rabbits, two hamsters and two goldfish.

What was your most embarrassing moment?
When I was in Year Seven I had to play piano for assembly. It was April Fool's Day and the piano wouldn't work (it turned out that someone had put a book in the back). I couldn't bring myself to stand up and investigate because that would draw attention to me, so I sat there with my hands on the keys wishing to die, until the Deputy Head came and rescued me!

To find out more about Ann Bryant visit her website: www.annbryant.co.uk

**For more fun and
friendship-packed reads
check out
www.fiction.usborne.com**